MW00441388

THE BREAK

DANIEL HURST

INKUBATOR
BOOKS

Published by Inkubator Books
www.inkubatorbooks.com

Copyright © 2022 by Daniel Hurst

Daniel Hurst has asserted his right to be identified as the author of this work.

ISBN (eBook): 978-1-915275-32-5
ISBN (Paperback): 978-1-915275-33-2
ISBN (Hardback): 978-1-915275-34-9

THE BREAK is a work of fiction. People, places, events, and situations are the product of the author's imagination. Any resemblance to actual persons, living or dead is entirely coincidental.

No part of this book may be reproduced, stored in any retrieval system, or transmitted by any means without the prior written permission of the publisher.

PROLOGUE

A ttending a crime scene is a difficult task for any police officer. There is no telling what might be waiting for them when they arrive. There is no way to know if the job will be routine or be one they will never forget.

It was no different for the officers who were assigned to visit 23 Churchill Road that sunny Monday in March. The house looked a mess from the outside. The officers climbed out of their vehicles and approached the property with apprehension. They had no idea what might be waiting for them inside.

The exterior showed signs of extensive fire damage, and while the blaze had been put out by firefighters the day before, the scene was still hazardous. That hazard would only increase the farther into the building the officers went.

The front door was undamaged. The officers used it to enter the building, taking care as they walked to avoid the charred wood and furniture inside. Treading carefully over the soot-covered carpet, the officers observed the grim scene before them.

This was not a fire that had started in one area and spread quickly throughout the property, like most house fires tended to do. There was no faulty electrical appliance to blame, nor was it due to carelessness on the part of one resident. Nor was it someone who forgot to turn off a gas hob or left a burning candle unattended. This fire had devastated each room, and the firefighters' report explained why that was.

Cause of fire: Arson.

As the police officers moved through the soot-blackened rooms, their feet crunching over bits of disintegrated furniture, they were all thinking the same thing.

They were glad this was not their house.

They were also stunned, yet again, by the deadly nature of fire.

They could not believe that this blaze had been started while people were inside.

But none of the officers were here to make judgements about the arsonist, or comment on their actions or what justified them. They were here to do a job. Together, they carried out that job efficiently, in the same way the fire had carried out its job of methodically destroying this building.

A couple of police officers went upstairs after being given the all clear from the firefighters. They looked inside the two bedrooms, as well as the bathroom, which had been the least affected by the fire.

The officers downstairs made sure to explore the kitchen, living room and dining room. Although, there wasn't much to see in these rooms; the fire had seen to that. The once-white cupboards that stored all the pots and pans were as black as the midnight sky. The sofas were now burnt-out shells covered in wet soot. All the books on the bookcase had been destroyed, as were the chairs that used to be around the dining table, and the painting that had hung in the hallway.

Everything was ruined down here.

Then one officer spotted something amongst the debris.

With a gloved hand, she plucked the item out of the mess. It seemed to be a book. At first guess, she presumed it belonged to the collection lost on the bookcase. But then she opened it and looked inside, and she realised it was not a book. This had several different messages written on the pages. The policewoman realised what this book was.

It was a guest review book.

That tied in with the incident report that mentioned this property was used as a holiday home.

The policewoman flicked through the book, expecting to see the usual things written inside it, like, *We had a lovely stay,* or *The property was lovely,* or *We will definitely be coming back here again.*

But this one had different messages, troubling ones.

Things like:

Your husband is a cheat.

You are so gullible.

The fire was not an accident.

But it was the last thing written that concerned her the most.

You will pay for what you have done.

1

KAREN

SIX WEEKS EARLIER

Is it normal to not want to go on holiday with your family?

I am mulling over the answer to that question as I make the short walk from my hectic household to the café on the street corner, where I am meeting my friend for a quick coffee and a catch-up. The reason I am deliberating over such a question is because my husband, Peter, suggested to me earlier that we should go away somewhere.

A holiday. All four of us.

Me, him, and our two children, Noah and Oscar, who, at eight and six years old respectively, are exhausting to look after on their good days and downright draining on their bad days. The prospect of organising my family enough to pack several suitcases and make it to the airport on time only fills me with dread.

That's why I told him I would think about it.

I could tell from his grim expression that my response was not expected. He probably thought he had come up with the best idea ever in suggesting we take a break. What wife doesn't want their husband to whisk them away somewhere a little warmer and sunnier, if only for a few days?

But some wives have second thoughts about family holidays, and I am one of them. I'm one of those wives who is old enough and experienced enough to know that sometimes going on holiday with the family is more taxing than staying put.

At thirty-eight, having been married for twelve years and with two unruly boys, I'm long past the point where holidays are relaxing. Or places where I get to recline on a sun lounger and sip alcohol through a straw for two weeks while working on my tan. Or places where the only thing I have to worry about is keeping the pages of my book dry beside the pool. Those holidays are the kind that would interest me, but with a family in tow, it is not the kind I would get.

If I was to take my husband up on his suggestion, then most likely I'd spend all my time chasing my children around, too afraid to let them out of my sight, worried about them burning in the sun or drowning in the sea. There would be more dramas than usual at mealtimes, because we would be eating in unfamiliar restaurants rather than at home. Never mind all the nights when my two overtired boys would refuse to sleep. Then, when the trip was over and I somehow managed to endure the journey home, I'd be left with the suitcases full of dirty washing to sort out. Never mind the dread that always followed, knowing it was almost time to go back to work.

If all of that sounds like a bit of a nightmare, then it's easy to see why I have my doubts. Maybe when the kids are a little older and can look after themselves more, I might consider it. Or better yet, when the kids have grown up, left home, and I can go back to spending my holiday the way I want –

thumbing through a good paperback while hubby sits at the bar.

But it's not just the hassle of holidaying with a young family that is making me disagreeable.

It's because I'm still coming to terms with what my husband did to me last year.

I walk along the frosty pavement, my coat wrapped tightly around me, shielded from the chilly February weather. But the shivers that occasionally run through me now are nothing compared to the ones I experienced on the night I found out my husband was having an affair.

It was a typical day in my life as a busy wife and parent. I was loading up the washing machine before making a start on that night's dinner. And that's when I found the receipt in Peter's trouser pocket. A slip of paper that unravelled the web of lies my husband had been spinning for quite some time.

The receipt was for a night's stay in a hotel in the town centre. While I had heard of the place, I hadn't stayed there before.

I had absolutely no idea why Peter spent a night at that hotel.

Checking the date in question on my calendar, I quickly realised Peter was supposed to be in London that night on business. Yet this receipt suggested he'd stayed in a hotel that was closer to home than the city. But why the lie?

I dreaded the answer to that question as I waited to hear the sound of his key in the front door.

When he arrived home, I was forced to delay my questioning of him for a couple of hours to feed Noah and Oscar. When those two eat, they devour food like a pack of wild animals. After I quenched their insatiable appetites, for a short while at least, I was finally able to confront Peter.

The shocked look that flashed across his face when I showed him the receipt said it all. But I waited for him to give me some kind of explanation, because at least that way I still had hope. When he fumbled and stumbled his way through a response, I knew he was telling me another lie.

Then came the excuses. He tried to make out that I had got my dates mixed up; he wasn't in London that night. But that still didn't explain why he chose to stay in a hotel a couple of miles from this house.

Then I came right out and asked him.

'Were you with another woman that night?'

'Yes,' came his reply.

I suppose I should be thankful that my husband was honest with me in the end. Some men would have clung onto a lie, any lie, to avoid admitting what they had done. But Peter didn't do that. He was decent enough to tell me everything. Although, he had waited until the kids were in bed and unable to hear what we were discussing.

Afterwards, we sat down together. I listened with tears in my eyes while he confessed to the affair he'd been having for three months. He told me he had met a woman in a bar while out with work colleagues. She had flirted with him, something he admitted no longer happened since getting older. The fact that he was the same age as me didn't occur to him. I am hardly ancient. I felt no sympathy for his plight, and even less after he admitted to swapping numbers with her and meeting her for coffee on his lunch breaks. Things progressed to sex shortly after that.

The fact he told me everything surprised me, until I realised I had done him a favour. I had lifted a weight off his shoulders. Peter said he felt guilty about what he was doing, and I actually believed him because I saw how open and raw he was being.

Then he continued his confession.

He told me that he'd visited her home four times, and

that the hotel stay was because 'she' wanted to go somewhere different with him.

'I could hardly have taken her here, could I?'

He added that he hadn't seen her since that night and had ended things with her. The woman begged him to leave his wife and kids and start a new life with her. He told her no. He told her he loved his family too much to lose them.

By the time all of that was disclosed, I almost felt like laughing, such was the hefty amount of adrenaline running through my body. The swarm of emotions in my body left me barely able to string a sentence together, let alone pack his bags and throw him out on the street. But what they did allow me to do was tell him I needed time to think about things, and he allowed me that time.

The fact we are still together tells you what I decided. I chose to stay, for my children's sake, so they could see their father every day. For his sake, because he was clearly sorry for what he did – although I have little sympathy for that. But also for my sake, because not only do I still love him, but I cannot bear the thought of divorcing and starting over as a single mum who is nearly forty.

Maybe my reasons for sticking with him aren't entirely right. Fear of being lonely is hardly the best reason for a couple to stay together. But I made my decision, and I am sticking with it despite how difficult it was over the last twelve months to forget and move on. Still is.

I honestly believe things are getting back to how they used to be between us, with a few exceptions. But I'm also aware that my lack of interest in his holiday suggestion could be another sign I'm not quite there yet. Maybe that's because it's almost easier to forget about what he did while I'm busy with school runs, work deadlines and emptying the washing basket. I worry that slowing things down, like what happens on a holiday, would make me think more about his affair, and I can't let that happen.

That's why I will keep discouraging the family holiday idea – if he brings it up again, that is. That doesn't mean I don't need a holiday. I really do. I just wish I could go away on my own for a few days.

A little break. By myself. Peace and quiet. No kids to clear up after. No husband trying to make up for what he did by being overly polite and keen.

Just me.

That's what I need. That's not too much to ask, is it?

That's the exact question I put to Eve in the café after ten minutes chatting over our cappuccinos. I expected sympathy from my childless and unmarried friend.

But I got more than sympathy.

I got the exact response I was looking for.

2

EVE

For the last ten minutes, I've been listening to Karen telling me how hectic her life is and how much she needs a break from it all. I stirred and sipped my coffee while she spouted more sob stories about how exhausted she feels and how she wishes she had a little time for herself. Apparently, meeting me for a coffee doesn't count as time for herself because after this, she has to get things ready at home for a birthday party tomorrow. She's only been able to grab this quick thirty-minute break while her husband drops the kids off at the local swimming pool.

It all sounds so draining. Hell, I'm feeling drained just listening to it.

But I am her friend, and I can't say I didn't know the drill when I agreed to meet her here. Karen never stops talking about how busy her life is. She's done so ever since I met her in the gym around the corner two months ago. We got to chatting one day while on the treadmill, both of us working through an exercise regime that was almost destined to fail before it even started. We got on well enough to take our chats to the café, and we have been meeting here semi-regularly ever since. Although, it's never easy to get Karen to commit to a time, on account of how busy she is.

Did I mention that she's a very busy woman?

Don't worry. Karen is sure to remind me of it again.

She barely pauses for breath. 'And then we have to go into the school and see Noah's teacher next week. Apparently, he's been acting up again in the mornings, during registration. That's the last thing we need.'

I nod, to show I agree that it is the last thing both she and Peter need. They have so much to do already. How will they ever find the time to fit one more thing in?

'Fingers crossed, everything seems to be better with Oscar these days,' Karen goes on. 'I mean, he's still a little terror at home, but what six-year-old isn't?'

On account that I don't have any kids of my own, I'm not able to add too much advice, but I try not to rub that reality in Karen's face. I don't want her to feel like my life is stress-free while she is drowning in a sea of dirty washing, discarded toys and a never-ending supply of meals. While I am neither in a relationship nor raising a child, I have plenty to occupy my time. In fact, I'm gearing up for a very busy period in my life, and pretty soon, I will barely have a minute to myself. But I haven't been given the chance to talk about my stuff today, because Karen is still going on about some other thing that is going to eat up even more of her time.

At least she hasn't mentioned Peter too much and that fling he had last year. I've heard enough about that to last me a lifetime. I was surprised that Karen confided in me about something so personal. I have never met Peter, nor do I think there will be plans for me to meet him, so I presume that's why she is comfortable enough to talk about him so openly. She probably thinks there's no risk of me saying something judgemental to him. But having heard all about how Karen debated whether or not to leave him, before ultimately deciding to stay, I have to say I prefer hearing about her kids more than I do about him.

Karen's busy life has not only told me a lot about her, but also given me an idea to ease some of her stresses and woes. If there is one woman in this world who needs a holiday, it is her. I know that she can be fun and witty at times when she is not so tightly strung, but those times have been few and far between. She definitely needs a break, and not just because she just told me.

That's why I've been waiting for the right moment to present my idea.

When I finally get a chance to speak in between one of Karen's breathless rants, I say, 'I wasn't going to mention it to you because I wasn't sure if it was something you would go for, but I think it might be just what you need. There's a holiday home not too far from here that I've stayed in. It's inexpensive and lovely and has great views of the country-side. It might be just what you need to get away from it all for a couple of days.'

I sit back in my seat, with one hand on my coffee cup, trying to gauge Karen's reaction to what I have just suggested. Will she go for it? I hope so, but that remains to be seen.

'You think I should go there on my own?' Karen said.

'Why not? I think a night or two away from everything is what you're crying out for.'

'But I can't just leave my kids.'

'It's hardly forever, is it? I'm sure Peter can manage until you're back.'

Karen still seems unsure, so I get more tactical, make it sound like it's something for me too.

'You have been talking about your family rather a lot,' I

say, trying to sound a little weary, but also good natured. 'I think a break would do you good.'

Karen suddenly looks mortified.

'Oh God, I *have* been talking about them a lot, haven't I? I'm so sorry, Eve. You must be bored to tears!'

I laugh off her remark, downplaying how bored I am with a gentle swipe of my hand and a simple shake of the head.

'No, I'm not bored. Not at all. But it's plainly obvious that you can't carry on like this without an outlet. What you need is some time for yourself. When was the last time you had that?'

Karen thinks about it for a moment, but the fact she is struggling to come up with anything gives me my answer.

'See what I mean? You're so busy looking after other people that you've forgotten to look after yourself. So how about the holiday home? It's cheap, it's local and, trust me, you'll leave feeling refreshed and revitalised. I know I do whenever I stay there, and I'm not half as busy as you are.'

As far as sales pitches go, I consider it a slam dunk, but I have to wait and see if Karen is really going to go for it, or if she is going to stall. But then a smile spreads across her face, and it looks like I might get what I want.

'Okay, I guess it wouldn't do any harm for me to look into it, would it?' Karen says. 'Is there a website for this place or something?'

'There's no website, but there is a leaflet,' I tell her. 'I've got it at home. I can give it to you the next time I see you.'

'A leaflet?' She laughs. 'What *is* this? The eighties?'

I chuckle before explaining this holiday home does business in a different way to most others.

'I think the owner doesn't want to get too booked up, so that's why she doesn't have a website. She prefers to keep it available for her regular customers. But I'm sure she'll be able to fit you in. Especially if you went during the week.'

'How did you find out about this place?' Karen asks as she picks up her coffee cup. 'It sounds very mysterious.'

'I heard about it from a woman at work. It does business on word of mouth only, which is usually the best form of advertising.'

'I've heard that too. I guess it works if you're telling me about it now.'

'I guess. Like I say, it is lovely, and it's very affordable. Just take a bottle of wine and a good book and relax and enjoy the views.'

'Wow, are they paying you a commission for this?' Karen jests, and I laugh.

'I wish. But sadly not.'

'Well, it does sound very tempting. I'm just not sure how I could get it past Peter. Telling him I am abandoning all my responsibilities for a couple of days is hardly likely to go down well.'

'Just tell him that it's something you need to do,' I say before mentioning a sore subject. 'Surely he can't grumble. Not after what he did.'

I pray I haven't pushed it too far. But Karen takes it well. She considers it for a moment, then nods her head.

'Okay, bring that leaflet next time, and I'll speak to him,' she tells me. I agree by clinking my coffee cup against hers, as if we were in a bar drinking something a little stronger.

By the time we finish our drinks and get up to leave, I'm feeling rather pleased with myself. I'm not sure how much better Karen is feeling, because she is already back to muttering about all the things she needs to get done. But that's not really my concern. All I needed to do was put the idea of the holiday home in her head. Now that I have, the next part of my plan for this woman is set in motion.

We hug outside the café before parting ways, but unlike Karen, I'm not rushing away because I have so many things I need to get home for. I'm just standing on the street, watching her go, in no rush at all.

There's a void in my life, and I am struggling to fill it.

But if everything goes to plan, I expect to be feeling much better about things very soon.

And Karen is going to be feeling much worse.

3

KAREN

If there is one time during the day when I feel like I can unwind, it is at 9pm. My sons are in bed, and I'm curled up on the sofa with the TV remote in my hand. Of course, I'm absolutely exhausted, and even just changing the channel is an arduous task. But at least the house is quiet. Peter is sitting on the opposite sofa to me, doing something on his laptop for work. I am mindlessly watching a reality show that anybody with two brain cells could follow.

I'm not sure if I would call it 'living the dream', but it's better than all the other things that happened today.

It started with Noah telling me he felt sick. Just a lame attempt to get out of another day of school, but he delayed me enough to make me late in dropping him and his brother off in the playground. Then, because I was running behind, I got stuck in the worst of rush hour, sitting in traffic for so long that I ended up being late to my desk and had to suffer several scolding looks from my boss. Lunchtime is usually a bright spot in my day, or at least it is when I actually remember to take my lunch to work. But I forgot it today, meaning I had to go out and buy an overpriced packet sandwich from the shop on the corner that does a roaring trade out of other worker bees like me.

Fortunately, my afternoons are much shorter than other nine-to-fivers because I have flexitime, which means I get to leave early to collect the boys from school. There used to be a bus service, but that stopped after it turned out that the school wasn't paying for the upkeep of the vehicle. It broke down one last time before being scrapped shortly afterwards.

After collecting Noah and Oscar and hearing all about their day, I drove them home. There, it was time to get on with some housework while plotting out what easy meal I could conjure up for later. The rest of the day whizzed by in a blur of pots and pans, of picking up food off the floor and washing up, then baths and bed. Peter and I actually had a minute to ask the other one how their day was.

It turned out to be a short conversation, because we were too tired to talk. Which leads us to this moment, where we are sitting apart on different sofas, and have been silent for at least fifteen minutes now.

I suppose if everything were all right between us, then I might not care about the lack of closeness and communication. I know many couples don't feel the need to talk all the time or sit next to each other when they watch TV. They just enjoy each other's company, speaking when they need to, offering affection when they feel like it, but otherwise just getting on with it.

But things are not all right between us, and they haven't been since Peter's affair came to light. That's why this distance between us and lack of conversation worries me. I did my part in accepting his infidelity, but Peter failed at his part. The fact that we aren't currently chatting and snuggling up together feels like just another consequence of his affair.

I look over at him on the other sofa, typing away on his keyboard. I suppose I could ask him what he's doing, but he'll just reply that he's sending an email for work. He'll know not to bore me with any more details, while I know better than to ask for them. I'm not really that interested in his job, just like he's not that interested in mine, so why pretend? Why force a conversation about work just for the sake of talking?

I try to think of something else we could talk about. Something that would be more fun. But fun is one thing that has been severely lacking in my life, so I'm struggling for some material. The only thing that does come to mind is the leaflet that Eve gave me yesterday, for the holiday home. I rarely go to the gym anymore, even though I'm paying thirty pounds a month for membership. But something made me put my trainers on and get in the car yesterday, just like something made me text Eve before that and ask her if she fancied a workout.

I have a strong feeling that the 'something' was so she'd give me the leaflet for the holiday home.

Despite my doubts about leaving my family for some *me time*, it is something I really want to do. But the leaflet is currently hidden in my handbag because I'm nervous about broaching the subject with my husband.

Perhaps tonight is the time to do that?

Or maybe I'll think about it a little more, leaving him to work in peace while I distract myself with nonsense on the TV.

I've just about managed to figure out what's been happening in the 'gripping' reality show when I hear a noise on the floor above. Peter hears it too, and he stops typing. We both look at each other and understand what it means.

One of the boys is out of bed.

'I'll go,' Peter says as he puts down his laptop and gets wearily to his feet.

'Thanks,' I say. Peter will put an end to any shenanigans going on up there.

I hear more footsteps as he climbs the stairs, followed by sounds of my husband talking to one of the boys, though I can't quite make out which son is in trouble. If I had to guess, I would say Oscar. He's the hardest to get to sleep after the lights have gone out. He proclaims to be a night owl, just like his mother, but that's only because he heard me say it once. Now he uses it as an excuse to run around and play games when he should be sleeping. But I suppose it could be Noah. He has been known to mess around at night too, and there have been a few times when I've caught him wide awake and playing with his toys.

But whoever it is, it becomes clear from the next sounds that it's not going to be a quick fix to get them back to bed. I hear Peter knocking on a door upstairs before a little voice shouts out, saying the four words that I have heard far too many times since we had our sons.

'I can't get out!'

With a deep sigh, I get up and head upstairs.

I join my husband outside the closed bathroom door that is between us and our trapped son.

'Why did you lock the door? We've told you not to do that!' Peter says.

'Oscar?' I whisper to my husband as he leans against the door with an exasperated expression on his face.

'Yep,' he confirms. 'I'll get my toolbox again.'

'I told you we need to change this lock,' I remind him as he goes, before trying the door handle and getting confirmation that it won't budge.

'How many times do we have to tell you the lock is broken on this door, Oscar?'

A sheepish 'sorry' comes from the other side.

It doesn't take long for Peter to return with his tools, and he takes out a screwdriver and unscrews the three hinges from the door. It's a simple process that only takes him a minute, but only because he has done it before.

The lock is always catching, which is why we tell Oscar not to use it. But does he listen? It's also why I told Peter countless times to replace it with one that is more child-friendly, so we don't have this charade every week, but did he listen to me either?

Of course not. It's like he takes pride in being 'man enough' to remove these door hinges; not having to do it in the first place would be better.

But I'm not going to argue with him about it tonight.

We've got enough problems on our plate.

With the hinges removed, the door is open, and Oscar is free. I take him back to his bedroom while Peter puts the door back. By the time all that is done, neither of us feels like going back to what we were doing before. We call it a night, heading for our bedroom, ready for some much-needed rest.

And so ends another day in the life of me and my family.

Typically chaotic, frustrating and tiring. I love my sons to bits, and I want to love my husband the same as I did before his affair, I really do. But right now, as I close my eyes and drift off to sleep, it is not them that I'm thinking about.

I'm thinking about the leaflet in my handbag.

I'm thinking about the holiday home.

4

EVE

I was disappointed when Karen didn't show at the gym tonight after giving her the leaflet a couple of days ago. I wanted to find out why she hadn't booked her break yet. I suppose her absence was kind of to be expected; when it comes to her fitness regime, she struggles to maintain any kind of routine. I guess a husband, kids and a job will do that to someone. I, on the other hand, was able to squeeze in a quick workout before returning home and getting started on my dinner.

I only work part-time for a local ad agency, which doesn't make me much money, but right now, my career and finances are the last things on my mind. But I appreciate that not all people like hearing about my whimsical life choices. That's why I told Karen that I work a standard forty-hour week at an office in town. She doesn't need to know it's a lie, just like she doesn't need to know about all the other lies I've been telling her.

At least not yet, anyway.

I stand over the pot of pasta bubbling away on the stove. It's taking me a little longer than it should do to make this standard meal. I'm still struggling to find my way around this unfamiliar kitchen.

I have to open three cupboards before I find the sieve, and it takes me two tries before I remember which one stores the cutlery. I really should know this by now; I've been living here for just over two months. But I don't always cook, often preferring takeaways that undo all the benefits I might have gained by going to the gym. Takeaways are also wiping out what little savings I have left, but as I said before, money is the last thing on my mind right now. I have bigger things on my plate – and I'm not referring to the pasta that I will soon devour.

After eventually getting my food ready, I take a seat at the small dining table and tuck in. Eating alone is never much fun, but eating alone in someone else's house is more depressing. I look around the room while I eat, seeing paintings I didn't pick, furniture I didn't fuss over, and a décor I didn't decide upon. But I'm not unhappy here, nor am I feeling out of place.

This may not be my home, but it *is* familiar to me.

It belonged to a dear friend.

I wish she were sitting at this table with me now.

I'm about halfway through my meal when I hear a crackling sound on the stove. I jump up to investigate and quickly realise that I left the gas on underneath my empty pasta pot.

'Damn it!' I say as I turn off the gas and grab the pot. In my haste, I forget the handle is hot, and I end up burning myself. I drop the pot into the sink with a clatter and run my hand under the cold water tap.

It stings, and tears fill my eyes. I soak it in the cold water some more to stop it from blistering. But the pain doesn't subside quickly enough, making my mood worse.

I pick up the pot and throw it across the kitchen, watching as it hits the wall on the other side of the room before clattering loudly onto the floor. The pan has left a dark mark on the wall. Regret fills me, but right now I have other things to worry about than cleaning it or picking up the pot.

I'm frustrated. I'm frustrated that I have been reduced to this.

Lashing out at inanimate objects. Eating alone every night. Being without my friend.

Plotting revenge.

'I'm sorry,' I say out loud, even though I'm alone. I turn off the tap and clean up the mess I made. By the time I'm finished, my meal is cold. I lost my appetite anyway, so I just go into the living room and slump onto one of the sofas.

The bookcase in the corner catches my eye. I wonder if I could lose myself in fiction for an hour or two. But I decide against the idea. Not because the books are not the genre I would read, but because I wouldn't be able to concentrate while I'm in this state of mind. I can barely put a meal on the table, get to sleep or make it through the few hours per day at my part-time job.

I'm a mess, and I can feel myself slipping more each day. But I just need to hold it together a little longer.

I need to see out my plan.

I don't care what happens to me after that.

I check my phone in case there is a text from Karen, requesting a stay at the holiday home. I'm disappointed when I see that I have no new messages. That's how it is these days. I don't get many texts. Not since my best friend died.

She was the only one who messaged me.

She was the only one I cared about messaging back.

All I care about now is some woman I barely know picking up her damn phone and making contact.

I need Karen to text me. I need her to tell me she wants to stay in the holiday home. If she doesn't, then I'm back at square one, and I'll have to find another way to screw with her.

But hopefully she will. I certainly sold the idea of this place enough for her to be tempted. I guess she just needs a little more time to make her final decision. But waiting is torture. I get up and walk over to the window.

The view out to the countryside, near the town where we both live, is spectacular. It's the same view I told Karen about. I just hope she is here soon, to see it for herself.

It will give her something to smile about. And she could definitely do with smiling.

Because by the time I'm done with her, she'll never smile again.

5

KAREN

My weary body sinks into the mattress, trying to draw me into what I hope will be a deep and satisfying sleep. But as so often happens after a frantic day, I find it difficult to switch off. My brain is still going at a hundred miles an hour, making sleep a struggle.

I'm the busiest person in the house. I'm the only one who isn't asleep.

I know that Noah and Oscar will be snoozing now, as it's gone midnight. If they were awake, they would have let me know about it already. I also know that Peter had no difficulty in dropping off tonight, because I could hear the sound of his light snoring coming from the spare bedroom. He's in there again because I asked him politely if he wouldn't mind giving me the bed tonight. I really need a good night's sleep, and there will be a better chance of achieving that without him wriggling next to me. He agreed, although he wasn't particularly thrilled about it. I think he hoped we were moving past separate rooms.

Him in the spare room was his punishment after I discovered his infidelity. He skulked into that room after telling me about his affair, told me to take as much time as I needed. But even that time has a limit. Now, he's done with being relegated to the spare bedroom. I can't say I blame him. It's been a while since the debacle, and things still haven't gone back to normal.

Not only are we not having sex, but we have to keep making excuses to the children when they ask why Mummy and Daddy aren't sharing one room. We'll often lie, tell them that Daddy was working late and didn't want to disturb Mummy. Excuses are easy to give at their age, and it isn't long before they become more interested in toys and what's for breakfast. But they must sense something isn't quite right. While they have no idea about their father's affair – nor do I ever want them to know about it – they aren't stupid. They must be picking up on the chasm between their parents that wasn't there before.

I roll over in the bed and stare at the empty space beside me. I think about how nice it would be for things to go back to normal: me watching Peter sleep whenever I struggle to; me reaching over to feel him beside me, giving me a deep sense of security; me getting kisses whenever he wakes first, his arm wrapping around me, making me feel safe and loved. There's no doubt that sleeping alone is very different to sharing a bed with someone. While I may have used the excuse of a better night's sleep, that's not why I sent him to the spare room.

I'm still struggling to mend what's broken between us.

And that's why I'm still struggling to sleep.

I let out a frustrated sigh. My brain refuses to quiet, so I turn on the bedside lamp before looking around for a book to read. I sometimes leave a paperback on my bedside table, and while I don't read every night, I like having it there in case I need a distraction before bed. But it's not there now, and I remember tidying up earlier and putting it back on the bookcase. Probably convinced myself I was never going to finish that particular story, so there wasn't much point leaving it next to my bed to collect dust. But I wish I had it now, or any book for that matter, because my mind is still whirring, and I need something to distract it.

Then I see my handbag.

There is something in there that I could read.

Stretching, I manage to grasp the handles of my bag and pull it towards me. Then I reach inside and take out the holiday home leaflet that Eve gave me.

I study the glossy paper in my hands that has a photo of the house on the front. Above it is stylised font describing this property as the ideal place for a 'short getaway'. The exterior is unremarkable but homely, not different from many other homes in this town. But what makes this one unique is the views. When I look out my window here, all I see are rows and rows of properties just like mine, all with cars and waste bins in the driveways. On the back of the leaflet is another photo of rolling, green fields, with the only neighbours appearing to be the fluffy kind dotted around in the fields. It really does look tranquil, and it's definitely the best view one could get around here without having to drive for a few hours or catch a flight.

As I lie alone in bed, staring at the leaflet and reading it over and over again, I make a plan. Eve wouldn't have recommended it to me if she didn't think it was what I needed.

Call today for a trouble-free stay.
No awkward check-in process. Just collect the key from the lockbox and you're good to go.
Stay for one night, or book two and get the second night at half price.

The longer I stare at this leaflet, the more tempted I am to go. But it's the last thing written on one side of the leaflet that makes my mind up.

Everyone needs a break. Now it's your turn.

It seems silly, but it almost feels as if the owner is talking to me. Of course, that is ridiculous. It's not a special message for me. Plenty of others will have read the same thing. But right now, the way I'm feeling, the message feels personalised. I guess that means it's good advertising copy and the owner knew just what to write. Anyway, I'm convinced. I decide to send an email right there and then.

It's almost 1am by the time I'm finished typing the message on my phone. I tell Sarah, the owner, that I am a friend of Eve's and she has recommended this place to me, and that I'm wondering about availability. I get ready to send it. But I hesitate for a moment, because I worry what the owner will think of my sending it at the unusual hour. Perhaps I should wait until the morning. But then I remember the chaos and commotion that is my morning. If I don't send it now, I might talk myself out of it.

I press send and smile at the idea of a night or two away in this lovely home with the sweeping views. I hope I can recharge my batteries and return home feeling refreshed, less exhausted and wanting to be a better wife.

Now the email is sent, there are only two things I can do.

The first is to try to get some sleep.

The second is to hope that when I wake up, I will have a reply from the owner telling me she is looking forward to arranging my stay.

6

EVE

It was the middle of the night when I noticed the email come through from Karen to the account I set up for this fictitious holiday home. The sight of it made me smile, and I was tempted to reply to it as soon as I finished reading it, but I made myself wait. It's more sensible to send a reply at a normal hour of the day, so that is why I am preparing my reply now, at 9am.

The fact she was awake and sending emails tells me she was struggling to sleep. I have some sympathy for her there because I suffer from the same problem. It's not insomnia, but I've been finding it tough to drift off at night. I put it down to me missing my best friend. I imagine that Karen's sleep issues stem from what Peter did, although it could be because she is so frazzled from raising those two children of hers. Either way, it seems we have one more thing in common. But that does not make me like her.

It just means she might be easier to manipulate. Sleep deprivation is hardly a recipe for making sound, sensible decisions.

I read through my reply several times, making sure it says

everything I need it to. Not only have I provided a few dates for availability, but I have also put a couple of extra details that will hopefully answer any questions she might have.

I tell Karen about the lockbox and how to access it, reminding her that the holiday will be a pain-free, easy experience. But the lockbox is also an excellent way to keep my identity a secret, ensuring that Karen will be none the wiser about the fact that she is being tricked.

Along with avoiding a face-to face for 'check-in', I also used a fake name on the leaflet. I am pretending to be 'Sarah', the owner of the holiday home, and there's no reason why Karen would suspect it to be a lie. Why would she? Her friend told her about this place in good faith. I even made the leaflet look legit. The email address is real, as is the information about the lockbox. Now all I need to do is find out what date she wants to stay here.

I press send and eagerly await her reply.

I presume Karen will be at work now, so I'm not sure how long I'll have to wait to get a response from her. She could be one of those good employees who doesn't check her phone until lunchtime, when she is technically 'off duty'. Or she may be one of those who doesn't care about rules and checks her phone at her desk. Or perhaps she might sneak away to the toilets to kill some time in one of the cubicles. We've all done it – time-wasting – because there's no greater enemy in work than the clock. But I will be ready whenever Karen chooses to get back to me, and I'm prepared to be patient. I've been patient thus far, so there's no need to rush. I can't risk this not working out like I planned.

KAREN'S REPLY arrives at midday. It suggests to me that she waited until her lunch break to reply. When I open it and read what she wrote, I'm frustrated to learn that she hasn't given me a firm date for her arrival. Instead, she confesses that she needs to have a chat with her husband this evening before she can confirm anything.

Yes, I get it. You need his permission before making your final decision.

I was hoping she would just book, but I guess it makes sense that she needs to run things by him first. He'll be the one looking after the children, so he'll need to be available.

But as I reply to Karen and tell her that is fine and I look forward to hearing from her soon, I feel a little anxious that Peter might throw a spanner in the works. What if he says no to Karen's idea of getting away for a day or two? What if he tells her that he needs her at home? Will Karen listen to him? Will she cancel her plans? If so, where does that leave me?

Back at square one, left to think up another plan.

That's why I really hope it doesn't come to that.

I pray that Karen will stick to the plan and not be swayed by any reluctance on Peter's part. After what he did to her, Karen is well within her rights to request time to herself. Plus, he's hardly one to make demands. That's why I'm confident this will go the way I want it to.

Even still, I decide to send Karen a text, to try to tip the odds back in my favour. This one will come from Eve, her loyal friend and confidante. I ask her how things are going in general before telling her Sarah has been in touch, thanking me for the recommendation. I do this, not only because it would make sense if it were true, but to put pressure on Karen to pursue her plans. I tell her in a roundabout way not to disappoint Sarah, because she is really looking forward to it.

Karen will hopefully feel guilty enough not to cancel any plans. Any cancellation will come back on Eve, her kind friend who suggested it in the first place. I know how to play her. I'm confident this tactic will improve my chances of her going through with it. For a little flair, I add in about how I am now entitled to a discount on a future stay at the holiday home myself because I drummed up a little extra business for Sarah. That should make Karen even more determined not to spoil things for me.

With the text sent, I sit back and wait. I don't expect to hear from Karen until later, after her chat with Peter. And I am hoping that it goes well, just like I imagine she is hoping for the same thing too.

But that remains to be seen.

After all, how many husbands would be happy for their wives to holiday on their own while leaving them to look after the kids?

7

KAREN

For someone who is sadly experienced in broaching awkward subjects with my husband, I'm still feeling unsure as to the best way to tell him about my plans. While this might be difficult, it pales in comparison to the conversation I had when I discovered he was lying to me. Yet I'm still struggling to speak to him, and it's why I waited until the kids were in bed and Peter is relaxing with a glass of red wine before I make any mention of it.

'I've been thinking,' I begin tentatively, to make it sound like I'm mulling it over rather than a final decision. 'There's this holiday home Eve told me about, which sounds nice, so I might book a short stay there.'

'Where is it?' Peter asks me, not taking his eyes off the TV.

'It's nearby. On the edge of town.'

'Wouldn't you want to go somewhere a little further afield?'

'I think it looks nice. And Eve really recommends it.'

'How much is it?'

'I've not got the final cost yet, but Eve says it's cheap.'

'Sounds like Eve is really selling this place.'

'She's just being nice.'

'Sure. Well, if you want to book it, then the boys and I will be happy with it. Have you got any photos?'

I realise then that my husband has misunderstood. Perhaps it's my fault because I haven't been clear enough, but he is under the impression that this will be a break for all of us. Sadly, I must burst his bubble.

'I was thinking of going by myself,' I say nervously. And that's when Peter looks away from the TV screen and at me, from the opposite sofa.

'What?'

'I need a break. Just a short one.'

'A break from what? From us?'

'No, not from us. Just from everything. Work. Housework. The kids. Life.'

'What are you talking about?'

This is not going as well as I hoped it would. I need to change tack quickly, or I might not get what I need. I'll not only be letting myself down but Eve and Sarah too.

'I'm exhausted,' I admit, deciding that brutal honesty is the way to proceed. 'But I'm not sleeping well. And I'm not sleeping well because I'm stuck in a rut, and every day feels like the same thing. Run around after the kids. Run around after you. Go to work. Come home from work. Tidy up. I never have a minute to myself, and even when I do it's not a break, because I'm still here, surrounded by all the other jobs I haven't got to yet.'

I see from Peter's expression that he is surprised at my spiel, but I go on before he has a chance to say something.

'I'm only talking about one night away. Two at most. And I'll still be nearby if you need me.'

I'm hoping that Peter will understand what I am saying, why I feel this is something that I have to do, and just give me his support. But he doesn't do that. Instead, he says the worst thing he could say at this time.

'Is this to do with what I did last year?' he asks me.

'What?'

'Is this because you're still mad at me? Is that why you want to get away? You're punishing me?'

'What are you talking about? How am I punishing you?'

'Oh, I don't know. How about leaving me to look after the kids, plus I still have to work, while you go and relax somewhere?'

'That's not what this is about.'

'Isn't it? Then why am I still being made to sleep in the spare bedroom every other night? Tell me that's not got anything to do with what I did.'

'Why are you bringing this up now? We said we wouldn't talk about it anymore.'

'Yes, we did, and I was happy with that arrangement after you accepted all my apologies. So why does it still feel like things haven't gone back to normal?'

This is the first time he has spoken to me about that time, and it's clear it has been weighing on his mind. I guess it's time for me to say a few things that have been weighing on my mind, too.

'Of course things haven't gone back to normal!' I say. 'You cheated on me. Did you think I would just forget about that?'

'No, but you told me we could work through things.'

'And that's what we're doing. I'm sorry if it's taking a little longer than you hoped for, but you broke my heart, so excuse me if I don't want to sleep next to you every single night, or if I need a night away just to have some personal time.'

'So when does it end – after this holiday? Or will you want to go away on your own more and more now?'

'No, this is a one-off. I just need a little break. I told you that!'

'So you need a break from me and the kids? How do we know you'll want to come back, or if you'll be doing it out of a sense of duty to us?'

'Of course I'll want to come back. I love the boys.'

'Do you love me?'

Peter's question hangs in the air, but it demands a quick answer, otherwise whatever I say after will fall flat.

'Yes,' I reply, and it is an honest answer. 'I do love you.'

That's the first time I have said those words to my husband since his affair. They are as surprising for me to hear as they are for him. But the fact that I said them placates him a little, and he seems less agitated now. Then he gets up from his sofa and joins me on mine, taking my hand.

'That's all I want,' he tells me. 'I'm sorry if I got angry or overreacted. I just want things to be normal between us again, even after the stupid thing I did.'

'I know that, and I want that too,' I tell him. It breaks my heart to see how raw and vulnerable he is being with me right now. 'I wouldn't suggest this if it wasn't something I needed to do, but I do need it. A little break from everything so I can get my mind straight, without all the noise and hassle of everything distracting me.'

Peter nods his head and then tells me he is happy for me to go for as long as I need. I assure him that it will only be a brief visit, and I might even cut it short if I'm missing him and the boys too much, but he tells me he will manage just fine without me.

It's a relief to have his support on this. Buoyed by it, I write another email to Sarah on my phone and propose a couple of dates out of the ones she gave me that work best. Peter goes back to drinking his wine and watching TV, but he remains next to me. It makes me feel good that we are sitting close rather than apart. I know I'll feel the same when he's sleeping beside me tonight. And I certainly know that we both feel relief after getting a few things off our chest.

But I also know that I will feel wonderful when I'm in that holiday home, relaxing in the quiet, peaceful surroundings without anybody demanding my time. No washing up. No cooking meals. No kids locking themselves in bathrooms. No husband with whom I am still working through my issues.

Just me.

A beautiful house.

And a few sheep.

Bliss.

So come on, Sarah. Hurry up and message back and confirm that I'm checked in.

8

EVE

Any good holiday homeowner should ensure the property is in excellent condition ahead of the next guest arriving. We don't want to disappoint the guest and attract a bad review. Therefore, my alter ego, Sarah, is busy making sure this house is ready for her first ever 'guest'.

I dusted every piece of furniture. I vacuumed all the carpets. I mopped the kitchen floor. And I scrubbed the bathroom until the porcelain was positively pristine. This house is as clean as it's ever going to get, and possibly cleaner than it has ever been before. I am confident that Karen will have no issues with the cleanliness. But making sure the property is tidy is just one part of what I need to do before my guest's arrival.

Having been on enough holidays myself over the years, I know that it is always a nice touch to leave out a few complimentary items to make the guest feel truly appreciated. That's why I put a bottle of champagne and a small box of chocolates on the kitchen table, where I know Karen will see them. They are right next to the review book that I have just filled with a dozen fake reviews.

I'm sitting at the table, in front of the champagne and chocolates, writing another fake review. No one has ever stayed here before, but I can't have Karen know that, which is why I'm making it appear as if there have already been dozens of satisfied guests.

Like Kelly from Kidderminster, who left a review saying, *I greatly enjoyed my stay. The home is lovely, and that view is to die for! Will definitely be back!*

Or Tiffany from Wigan, who wrote, *This house is beautiful. Thank you Sarah, and I can't wait to stay here again.*

But my personal favourite has to be the review from Megan from Manchester, who described this holiday home as, *The perfect place to get away from it all for a couple of days,* before adding that, *I could stay forever, but I have a family to go back to. But next time, I'll be bringing them all with me!*

I like Megan's 'review' the best, because not only does it give this home a glowing endorsement, but it will also hopefully prime Karen for what I want her to do – bring her own family here to stay. As far as a piece of propaganda goes, this book is certainly powerful.

I put down my pen and flick back through the pages to do a final check over all the fake reviews I wrote. I am satisfied that I accomplished what I needed to. It was hard work and time consuming having to alter my handwriting to make each one appear legit. But I feel like I did a good job, and Karen will not suspect a thing.

To further improve my chances of her believing this lie, I made sure to add a couple of minor criticisms, like the irritating sheep bleating at dawn, or that there could have been a wider selection of paperbacks to choose from. Just like the tidy surroundings and the goodwill gift, this review book will be expected.

Done, I sit back and look around, confident I am ready. Now all I need to do is send Karen a quick message to say that the house is set for her arrival, and that I wish her an enjoyable stay. I take out my phone and do just that.

For the Tuesday and Wednesday evening that Karen requested, I quoted her £150, which I thought was more than reasonable, especially when I compared the price to other holiday homes in the area. They were much more expensive, and some didn't look half as nice as this house. After Karen accepted the fee, she asked me how she could make payment. I told her I would prefer it if she could pay in cash, and that I was happy for her to leave the money in an envelope next to the review book just before she checked out.

That might seem trusting of me, but knowing my guest as well as I do, I know there is no way Karen will not pay what she owes. Doing it this way means I don't have to set up a new bank account and struggle with all the complications that would come with running a fake business under a fake name. Thankfully, Karen told me that cash was fine. I'm sure she presumes that I might want the money under the table, to avoid the taxman, but it's not her place to judge me.

She just wants a break from life.

And here, she is going to get it.

I'm at the point where I'm feeling so smug with myself that I almost forget to do something important. Something that could potentially mess everything up if I neglect to do it before Karen arrives. I hurry outside, scurry to the end of the driveway and pull the 'For Sale' sign out of the flowerbed.

Karen might have been a little puzzled to see such a sign, and it might have led to a few doubts about staying here. I could, of course, explain that the property is on the market but can be used as a holiday home until then. But by removing the sign, I am removing as much doubt as possible of Karen discovering the truth about this place.

The truth is that this house is currently for sale, and that it has been for a couple of months. The owners put it on the market after receiving it in my best friend's will. The owners are Leanne's parents, my late friend. They have been letting me stay here for free since her death because they know me, trust me and are helping me get over her loss as much as I have tried to help them. But the time has come for them to move on from this place. Leanne's mum and dad are hoping for a quick sale, and when they get it, I will be expected to live elsewhere.

Considering what a lovely area this house is in, and the fact that I only work part-time, there is no chance of me acquiring this home for myself. The only people who can afford places like this are the couples with two incomes, or affluent singles. Leanne fell into that latter category. But her parents aren't just letting me stay here out of the goodness of their hearts, even though they are both kind people. I promised to show the place whenever prospective buyers called around to see the property.

At least that was the plan, anyway.

But so far, I've been doing as little as I can to get this place sold, from cancelling viewings to giving half-hearted tours of the house – whenever somebody does manage to make it inside, that is. I tell lies about the place, like how nice the fresh country air is, if you don't mind the stench of manure that goes with it. Or about how difficult it is to get a good Wi-Fi connection in a house this old, which puts off professionals or those with kids, who might need to work from home.

So far, I have done a good job of not only putting off anybody keen to make an offer, but in keeping Leanne's parents in the dark about my sabotaging efforts. But I am aware that I won't be able to keep it up forever, because they are already getting suspicious of why there have been no offers. I don't need to delay it forever. I just need enough time to do what I need to do to Karen and her family. Then I will leave this place and never look back. Now that Karen is on her way here, that time is getting closer.

After hiding the sign down the side of the house amongst some hedging, I lock the front door and leave a spare key in the lockbox, where I already told Karen it will be. Then I walk away, but as I do, I check on something.

I check that the hidden cameras in the house are broadcasting footage to my mobile phone.

They are.

That means I will be able to see Karen as soon as she arrives.

9

KAREN

fter all the deliberating over whether I could leave my loved ones and my responsibilities behind, as well as the back-and-forth messages with Sarah to confirm my stay, it's a relief to finally take the key out of the lockbox.

I prepare to step inside the holiday home. Now that I'm here, I feel as ready as I can be for a break. I cannot wait for two days of peace and quiet with nobody to look after but myself. I'm sure that by the time I leave here, I'll return home a more relaxed, productive and sympathetic mother and wife than when I left.

I could say that I'm not just doing this for me but for my family too. While that might be stretching it a little, I do honestly believe they will see my getting away as the best thing for our family in the long run.

Turning the key in the lock, I push open the front door, then bend down to pick up my small suitcase that I carried from the taxi that dropped me off here. I didn't pack much considering I'm only here for two nights, but my suitcase seems to be fuller than I intended. I ended up bringing way more than I need.

But so what? I'm on holiday on my own. That means there is no one here to judge me. Peter usually grumbles whenever we go away together and he sees how much I brought. But this time, he's picking up the kids from school while I'm doing as I please. Perhaps now, he might appreciate just how much I do for the family when he's not around.

My first thought when I enter the home is that it is clean and tidy. I gather that not only from the polished surfaces and clean carpets, but because my nostrils are hit with the scent of bleach and air freshener. Sarah really has done her best to make this holiday home ready for my arrival. As I put down my suitcase and explore a little more, I really appreciate it.

My first port of call is the living room, where I immediately spot the bookcase full of paperbacks that Eve told me was here. I also see a couple of titles that I might be interested in flicking through at some point during my stay. But it's the window next to the bookcase that is drawing my eye. I go there, eager to see the view, as per the leaflet. When I do see it, I'm not disappointed.

The photo doesn't do it justice. It is truly stunning. I gaze out over green fields, spotting sheep, and smiling to myself as I take it all in. It's hard to believe that I get to enjoy a view like this, and all for a very affordable rate.

As I step away from the window, I am thinking two things. One, I'm glad I booked two days so I could really relax, and two, I must send Eve a text message shortly and thank her again for telling me about this place.

But before I can take out my phone and type a message to my friend, I see something in the kitchen. There is a bottle of champagne and a box of chocolates on the table, alongside a note from Sarah wishing me a lovely stay and telling me to help myself to the treats.

It doesn't take me long to tear into the chocolates and stuff a couple into my mouth. Then I remember these are all mine, so I don't have to be so quick when it comes to getting my share of food.

I'm just about to go in search of a champagne flute in one of the many cupboards when I see the book sitting on the table next to the champagne. I take a seat and open it, then read a few of the reviews inside. The more I read, the more I see that this place has been enjoyed by many people before me. All the reviews are extremely positive, bar a couple of silly comments about noisy sheep and the choice of books on the bookcase. It seems everyone who stayed here before was happy they came. My stay might only have begun, but I already know I will be adding my very own review to this book, and it will be just as positive.

After popping open the champagne and pouring myself a glass, I continue my exploration. It takes me down into the basement, where I check out the movie room that Eve told me about. A door with an old-fashioned hook latch leads me into a room, kitted out with a comfy sofa in front of the large TV screen on the wall. The lack of windows down here makes it the perfect place to spend a cosy night in watching a film. I figure this used to be an old cellar that was converted, and it's definitely a good use of space. I decide to return a little later and make the most of it, once I get settled upstairs.

On the top floor, I find one extremely clean bathroom and a couple of bedrooms. I put my suitcase down on the biggest bed and start unpacking, knowing that this task is all that stands between me and a relaxing couple of days. It doesn't take me long to transfer most of my things out of my suitcase and into the dresser. I put my toiletries by the sink in the bathroom and go back downstairs.

I can already feel the tension leaving my body as I flop down onto the sofa in the living room. I consider taking a little nap. It almost seems silly to waste time when there's an amazing view, a great selection of books, a movie room all to myself, and the rest of the chocolates. But as my eyes drift closed, it's all I want to do.

I AM surprised when I open my eyes again and see that an hour has passed. I actually napped. That is very rare for me. But it's so quiet here, and this sofa is so comfortable. I sit up, and suddenly I'm worried that two days won't be enough.

I already feel like I want to stay here forever. I wonder how much a house like this would cost to buy. It surely can't be cheap with that view, not that anybody who owned a place like this would want to sell it. It's too unique, and as far as it being a holiday home, I wonder why Sarah doesn't charge more for a night's stay. This place could be a goldmine if she hiked her prices up. But I'm not going to complain. I have her money in an envelope in my bag, ready to leave behind when I check out. I also put an extra £20 in there as a tip, because so far I have not seen anything that makes me think such a tip is not warranted.

I'm tempted to grab a paperback from the bookcase and while away the next hour with a little reading. Before I do, I take out my phone and write a message to Eve. I thank my friend for telling me about this holiday home and say that it's already proving to be just what I need. Then I press send and put my phone down, determined not to pick it up again unless Peter or one of the kids calls me. I'm not expecting any dramas, but there could be a situation where my husband is making dinner and has no idea which drawer the spatulas are kept in, or one of the boys is looking for a toy and can't find it in the same place I always put it after tidying up after them.

If there are no emergencies today, I will call home before the kids are put to bed and tell them that I love them. I will tell Peter that everything is fine and not to worry. And that will be it.

No Noah or Oscar running around after lights out and locking themselves in the bathroom. No tossing and turning in my bed after another lousy night of sleep, thinking about all the errands I have to do the next day. Definitely no racing around in the morning to get the boys to school before hitting rush hour and trying to get to work on time.

It's just me, this lovely house and nothing else.

Peace and privacy.

What more could a woman want?

10

EVE

I think about all the things I've ever wanted in my life. Love. Commitment. Security. Then, remembering I have none of them, nor am I likely to get them, I stop wasting time thinking about things I can't control and focus on the one thing I can. That's why I look at my mobile phone and the surveillance footage of the house.

Karen is in shot, soaking in a bubble bath, her eyes closed, her head resting against the side of the tub. She looks relaxed, and why wouldn't she be? She's got the whole house to herself, and she doesn't have to answer to anybody. I already watched her enjoying the complimentary champagne and chocolates I left behind, as well as seeing her take a nap not long after she checked in. She certainly wasn't lying when she told me she was tired. Now she is enjoying a mid-afternoon bath, and who knows what she is going to do after that?

Sit outside and enjoy the view? Thumb through a book? Watch a movie? Snoop around in some drawers?

It's not clear what she will opt for next, but whatever she decides to do, one thing is for sure.

I will be watching.

Looking up from the screen, I check the street ahead for any sign of the other person I'm interested in keeping tabs on today. But he's not here yet – not that I'm unprepared to wait. For now, I will remain on this street corner, tucked behind this parked car that I can use should I need to duck behind it. But I'm not expecting I'll have to, because I am a safe distance away from the primary school. There are plenty of other people around here to make me unseen.

The reason for the crowd is that the bell has just rung. That means all the pupils will soon be pouring out of the classrooms and rushing towards whoever has come to collect them.

The line of mums and dads, grandmas and grandads, uncles and aunties, babysitters, family friends and so on is a big one.

But the one adult I am hoping to see here today has not shown yet. When I see the school gates open and the youngsters in uniforms flood out, I realise that Peter is late.

Having watched Karen enough times, I know she is never late. The fact that Peter has failed to turn up on time for his first school collection reflects badly on him. I get that he probably had to leave work early to be here today, but even so, it's not asking much for a father to be here for his children, is it?

As the swarm of schoolkids rush out onto the street, I watch the excitement register on several little faces when they see their loved ones. They run towards them, eager to share stories about their day, eager to get home as quickly as possible, where snacks are surely waiting. It's then I see Noah and Oscar exiting the school, and they don't look quite as excited.

They look unsure as they search for their dad.

I keep my eyes on the two boys standing by the gates. The

crowd around them starts to disperse, and there is still no sign of Peter. Has he forgotten them? Is he still sitting in his office? How long until he remembers where he's actually supposed to be? And will the school have to call him to remind him of his parental duties?

As amusing as I'm finding the spectacular failure of Peter's first school collection since Karen's break, I am also a little concerned that he might not be whom the school calls. What if they call Karen instead? Will she leave the holiday home and come down here to get them? I'm certain she would. There's no way she would leave them waiting any longer than necessary.

But I don't want that to happen. I want Karen to stay put because I have something planned, and it will be a lot easier to do it with her out of the way. But if Peter doesn't show up soon, then things might get a little tricky.

Peter suddenly arrives by car and pulls up outside the school. Noah and Oscar see their father waving to them and head towards the vehicle. The two boys get into the car, and Peter drives away.

Problem solved.

Karen won't be getting any phone calls from the school, and she doesn't have any reason to cut short her holiday. I'm pleased about that as I check my phone again to see what the woman is up to now. She's still in the bathtub, enjoying her relaxing afternoon, blissfully unaware of how late her husband was to collect the kids.

I wonder what Peter's excuse to his kids was for being delayed. If I had to guess, I'd say he blamed it on the traffic. But whatever his reason, he's on his way home with the boys now, and that means I can make my way over there too. That's because I'm planning on paying Peter a little visit this evening. I want to catch him alone, without Karen there, so we can talk more freely. I imagine a man like him, given his past indiscretions, must be very careful about how much time he spends chatting to other women. He'll know not to do anything that could ramp up Karen's paranoia. But with Karen out of the picture for now, I'm hoping he won't be so nervous around me when we finally get to talk later.

I've never met Peter before. We've never spoken, and I know he won't have seen any photos of me, because I made sure to close down all my social media accounts before I befriended his wife. I expected she would go snooping for me online and show me off to her hubby. But today is the day that Peter and I will become a little more acquainted.

Although I won't be introducing myself as Eve, his wife's friend. I'll be someone else entirely, another fictional character just like Sarah, only my new persona has a different intention. While Sarah existed to seduce Karen away from her home, my next alias will be playing a different type of seduction.

She will flirt with Peter. She will make him feel good about himself. And then she will get inside his home while his wife is away.

Will she succeed? Based on Peter's history, I'd say there is a good chance of that.

Whatever happens, it promises to be fun, and I feel like I deserve a bit of that.

Karen is enjoying herself.

Now it's my turn.

11

KAREN

My skin feels soft and smooth after soaking in the bathtub for almost an hour. Now that I'm out of the water and dry, I'm ready for the next part of my relaxing day. It's hard to believe it's five o'clock on a weekday. At this time, I'm usually feeling burnt-out after work, after having collected the kids and gotten their dinner ready. Instead, I'm wandering around this quiet holiday home, wearing a fluffy, white dressing gown and wondering how to spend the first part of my evening.

It's already gone dark, thanks to the British winter, so I'm no longer able to enjoy the view. But I console myself that it will be there again when the sun rises. But now, I find myself in front of the bookcase, perusing the many reading options.

After taking my time, I decide on a crime thriller from an author I haven't heard of before. The blurb on the back cover intrigues me enough to make it my first pick. With the paperback in hand, I curl up on the sofa and open to the first page, making sure the box of chocolates is close to hand.

I haven't got a plan for dinner, but Sarah mentioned that the local takeaways all deliver, so I guess I can just call one of them when my hunger outgrows the chocolates. This is a holiday. I'm not going to feel guilty about ordering something unhealthy, nor am I going to feel guilty about eating without sharing. How often do I get to do something like this? Never, and I'm not sure if I'll get to do it again. I can't get into the habit of going away alone. It's hardly fair to Peter or the kids to keep doing it, so I plan to make the most of the break.

The book is as enjoyable as I predicted, and I manage to lose myself in the story. By the time I look up from the book, I see it is past six o'clock now. Despite my enjoyment, I still can't stop thinking about my family's day. Routine is a big part of our lives, which means that even though I am not there with them, I can easily figure out what they are doing and when.

By now, the boys should have had their dinner. It won't be long before they are getting ready for bed, so that gives me a small window to call and check in, to see how they are all doing. I know this was supposed to be a break from motherly and wifely duties, but that doesn't mean I don't miss them. A simple phone call is hardly going to leave me riddled with stress.

At least I don't expect it to, anyway.

Picking up my phone, I call Peter's number, expecting him to answer right away. I think about how it will be nice to hear his voice before he passes the phone over to the boys. But it just keeps ringing, and I give up after the sixth ring. He probably didn't hear my call. He will return it shortly.

I put my phone down and pick up the book again, trying not to read too much into Peter's failure to answer. He could be busy with the boys, perhaps helping them with their homework. Or maybe he just left his mobile in his work trousers upstairs, as he sometimes does after he gets changed.

He'll call me back soon. Until then, I'll just enjoy this book.

But getting back into the story proves impossible, and I realise I won't relax until I hear from Peter and know that everything is okay. I guess this is the fatal flaw in my plan to call them. Despite needing the break, there's no remedy for the fact that I simply miss my family and want to know they are okay. It's the gift and curse of motherhood. The gift is that I get two little lives to love and cherish, but the curse is that I can never really rest, either with or without them, because I will always wonder what they are up to and if they need me.

I try Peter again five minutes later, but there's still no answer, so I send him a text message asking him how his day is going. I decide not to mention what I have been up to, in case he has been having a nightmare. But waiting for a reply is as tedious as waiting for him to pick up his phone.

I get up and go somewhere else in the house, to stop myself fretting for another few minutes.

I decide to go down to the basement and see if I can find a movie to watch. I descend the short staircase and open the door that leads into the cinema room. The big sofa is appealing, but I stay standing as I pick up the remote control and turn on the flat-screen TV, then flick through the film options. I keep my phone in my other hand just in case Peter calls. But by the time I decide on a rom-com movie, there is still no response from him.

Settling on the basement sofa, I watch the opening credits for the movie. The rom-com was the more sensible option than one of the horror movies, seeing as I'm home alone. I played it safe with some fluffy film about two people who get chatting in a coffee shop and fall in love after several 'hilarious' trials and tribulations.

But the lack of a response from Peter is still bothering me, and it's only when I check my phone for what must be the tenth time that I realise something.

There is no signal down here.

I guess this basement isn't the best place to receive calls or texts.

Pausing the film, I go back upstairs, where I stare at my phone until I see the signal strength return to full. As soon as I get it, I wait for a notification to flash up, telling me that Peter has either tried to return my call or has left me a message.

But there is still nothing.

Why isn't he getting back to me?

Is everything okay?

Or am I going to have to rush home and check on my family?

I don't want to cut my holiday short, because the whole point of coming here was to have a break. But it's not much of a break if I'm worrying, and now I am. Not even another chocolate can calm me down.

I knew this was a bad idea. I knew I should have just got on with things. What kind of person wants to leave their family for a few days, then actually goes ahead and does it?

Me.

Does that make me a bad person?

Maybe.

Or perhaps I'm just being paranoid. Unfortunately, after what Peter did to me last year, paranoia is now an old friend of mine.

12

PETER

'Dad, that's not how you do it.'

The statement from Noah does not fill either of us with confidence about my ability to get a semi-appetising meal on the table. The truth is that I have been trying, and mainly failing, to cook fish fingers, chips and beans for the last half an hour. Thanks to my distinct lack of know-how of cooking, it's proving to be a bit of a struggle.

Noah has just pointed out yet another mistake in operating the oven, which probably explains why the fish fingers and chips are still not ready.

'I think Mummy presses this one,' my eldest son tells me as he touches one of the many electronic buttons on the oven. It makes a bleeping sound before the light flicks on inside the oven. Hopefully, that means the cooking has resumed, but I can't be sure because, rather embarrassingly, I've never actually used this oven.

Rightly or wrongly, Karen has always done the cooking. It's not because I'm a chauvinistic pig who feels above doing any kind of menial task. It's simply because she is good at it, and I am absolutely useless. I can barely make myself a crisp sandwich, never mind cook a hot meal, so it's no surprise that the first night without my wife has led to a bit of a dinner disaster. If it were up to me, then I would order a takeaway, but Karen said that would be cheating and challenged me to make something – anything. I accepted that challenge, hoping to prove I can be left alone to feed the kids. But that challenge is overwhelming me now. It's only the help of my two children that has got me this far.

'See, the timer is back on now,' Noah tells me, as if he is the experienced chef, and I am the kid on work-experience, which isn't far wrong, if I'm honest. 'Just don't touch anything until it beeps again.'

Noah's latest instruction says it all about how confident he is in my ability.

I do as he says and step away from the oven, hoping it will tell me when the food is ready rather than me having to figure it out.

As I look away from the oven, Oscar comes running into the room wearing his school sweater and nothing else.

'What are you doing? Where are your trousers?' I ask the six-year-old. He scurries around the kitchen table before running back out of the room again.

I know I could go after him and make him put on clothes, but I also know it will most likely be a tedious, drawn-out event. So I decide to leave it for the moment and focus on my next job.

'We need plates,' I say to myself, planning ahead.

I open one cupboard door where I know the plates are, but I'm surprised when I see that the cupboard is empty. The plates definitely used to be kept here. Even someone as useless as me in the kitchen knows where the plates are kept. So why aren't they here?

'Why haven't we got any plates?' I ask Noah, who is sitting

at the kitchen table and trying to get on with his maths homework again.

'They'll be in the dishwasher,' Noah replies, not looking up from his textbook. He answers with all the weariness of someone a lot older than him.

'Oh, right,' I say, grateful for his suggestion. Otherwise, I would have resorted to opening every cupboard.

After unloading the dishwasher, I get some idea of why Karen is always looking harassed whenever I get home from work. It's certainly not easy trying to get things done while looking after two young boys.

School runs. Homework. Dinner.

And that's all before bed, a routine that I am dreading, because that's an ordeal even with two parents. I'm becoming more aware of how busy this house can be while I'm not here. I'll try to get home a little earlier so I can help. Until she returns from her break, I've still got a little while to go before normality returns to my life or that of the kids.

But no matter how much I might struggle without her, one thing I will not do.

I will not call my wife and ask for advice or, worse, beg her to come home.

I need to show her I am more than capable of managing by myself, and that our whole family won't fall apart if she goes away. The fact she needed a break from everything galled me a little. It told me about how exhausted she must be to suggest such a thing. I know how much she loves the boys and hates being apart from them. I'm just ashamed that I didn't notice her stress before she brought it to my attention. But her request for time away worried me for another reason. I feared it had to do with the heartbreak I caused her.

As frenetic as my life is right now, I'm also grateful to still be in this house, to still have my wife and my children. Karen would have been within her rights to kick me out and divorce me after what I did to her. I am grateful that she gave me another chance. I know I made a dreadful mistake, and I know I risked losing the three people who matter most to me in this world. But thankfully I am still here. I need to keep working hard to ensure that doesn't change.

But I won't make the same mistake twice. I'll never get involved with another woman again. Not just because it's a normal rule for a married man, but because I have first-hand experience of the devastation it can cause. I'll never forget the look on Karen's face when I told her about my affair.

It was a stupid mistake that saw me get caught in the end. But I'm grateful for it because it brought that silly affair to an end. I'd been meaning to stop seeing Leanne long before I actually did. Leanne wanted me to leave my wife, but I knew deep down that I would never do that. It was my fault. I led her to think that we might have had a future together. That is another cause for my shame, but I am certain I did the right thing, choosing to stay and make things right with my wife.

Leanne worshipped me. At least, she did until I told her I was choosing Karen over her.

The sound of the oven beeping breaks me from my thoughts. It gives me hope that this dinner might finally be getting somewhere. When I open the door to check on the hot food inside, it certainly looks cooked. But Noah gets up from the table and joins me, to offer his expert opinion. I'm happy to receive it, because there are things in this house he knows far better than me.

Warming beans in a pan is one task I can handle, so it doesn't take long after the chips and fish fingers are done before I'm able to serve dinner. I'm glad to see that Oscar has put on trousers, although I'm not thrilled to see more food on his school sweater than in his mouth.

'Don't talk with your mouth full,' I have to remind him, which I figure is the reason for the mess.

Oscar and Noah chat to each other while they eat, talking about some new video game that I have never heard of. I don't have much to add to the conversation, and I'm happy to eat my meal quietly for a few minutes. The occupied pair allows me a moment to check my phone.

I haven't looked at it since I got home from picking up the boys from school. I have several missed calls and messages from Karen.

I worry that something is wrong, but then I read one of her texts and see that she is just checking in. I put down my fork to reply and put her mind at ease, telling her that the boys are fine, we're all just eating dinner, and I will call her when we are done.

'Mum says no phones at the table,' Oscar rather kindly reminds me.

'Mum's not here. Eat your food,' I reply, finishing my text message and pressing send before returning to my meal.

But I don't get a chance to finish it before I hear a knock at the front door.

'Who is that?' Oscar asks.

'Is Mum home?' Noah wants to know.

I don't answer as I get up from the table and go to the door.

I have no idea who could be calling at this hour. I'm certainly not expecting anybody. If I had to guess, I'd say it is a door-to-door salesperson who spotted my car in the driveway and decided to take a chance. Someone probably looking to sell me cheaper energy rates or something else I don't need at this time.

But when I open the door, I see it's not a salesperson with a clipboard, ready to break into some sales spiel.

It's an attractive woman.

And she is smiling at me.

13

EVE

I smile widely at the man in the doorway eyeing me up and down. I'd like to think it's because he's attracted to me, which I suspect he is, but it's also likely he is trying to figure out why I just knocked on his door.

'Hi. Can I help you?' Peter asks me, not quite smiling yet, although I bet I can rectify that shortly.

'Hi. I'm sorry to bother you. I hope I'm not interrupting anything?'

'Er...no, it's fine.'

Peter glances over his shoulder, but doesn't seem in a rush to get back to whatever he was doing.

So I go on.

'My name's Natasha, and I've just moved into the area,' I say, giving another fake name, because they work well to deceive. 'I'm just going around to a few houses to say hello. I hope you don't mind. It's just that I'm new to the area, and I don't know too many people, so I'm trying to be neighbourly.'

'Oh, right. I see,' Peter says, still looking a little sceptical. But I feel his scepticism is probably because he thinks it's rare for people to introduce themselves to every neighbour rather than because he doesn't believe my story.

'It's nice to meet you…' I say, holding out my hand. I wait for him to tell me his name.

'Peter,' he replies, shaking my hand. 'Nice to meet you.'

I don't release his hand straight away. I want him to think that while I am just being friendly, he could mistake it for something else too.

I hold Peter's gaze, and my smile doesn't fade, not even when we release each other. I wonder how that moment made Peter feel. Did he enjoy it?

He likely did. He's a man, I'm a woman, and despite him being married, he is still human.

'So is it just you living here?' I ask, looking around his hall as if I have no idea of the answer.

'Oh, erm, no. It's me and my family,' Peter replies honestly.

'That's nice. Are they in?'

'My sons are, but my wife is out.'

'Oh, that's a shame. It would have been nice to meet her. Maybe next time.'

I make sure that my seductive look lets Peter know I'm not that disappointed about his wife's absence.

'So, erm, which house have you just moved into?' Peter asks me, breaking what was quickly becoming an intense moment between us. He casually looks down the dark street, as if trying to spot where I might live.

'It's just round the corner. I moved in a couple of days ago, but the neighbours closest to me are all a little…how do I put this politely…ancient.'

Peter laughs, and I know I have just become more endearing to him. Humour always does that. A woman can't rely on her good looks alone, can she?

'Yeah, there's quite a mix of generations around here,' he tells me, leaning against the doorframe. His casual stance tells me that he is not in any rush to end this conversation yet. 'But you'll be pleased to hear that there are a few younger families around here too.'

'How about some young singletons?' I ask cheekily, and Peter looks a little caught off guard.

'Oh, erm. I'm not sure. I guess there will be.'

'I'm sure I'll find them. I can't imagine they're hiding.'

I smile again, waiting for Peter to continue the conversation, because I'm curious as to what he might say next.

'So are you on your own?' he asks me, which is a less obvious way of asking me if I am single.

'Yeah. It's just me. That's why I'm doing this, to maybe try to make a new friend.'

'I see. It's a shame my wife isn't in. You two might get along quite well. You're a similar age.'

'How old do you think I am?' I tease.

My question is designed to make Peter feel uncomfortable. What man likes having to guess a woman's age, particularly one he is subconsciously trying to impress?

'Erm, I don't know, actually,' Peter mumbles.

'Don't worry, I'm not going to make you guess a number,' I tell him with a chuckle. 'Unless you want to say twenty-one, then I'll happily accept that.'

Peter laughs again, enjoying another one of my jokes. While it's clear I am much older than twenty-one, making such a suggestion will make me seem more youthful to him. That's important, because I wonder how many times Karen makes herself seem youthful.

'Yeah, it would have been nice to meet your wife,' I go on. 'Although I do tend to get along better with men for some reason. Most of my friends in the last place I lived were guys.'

'Oh, really?'

'Yeah, it's always been that way for me ever since I left school. I guess being a beer drinker and liking football means I have a little more in common with the opposite sex.'

Peter's brows lift. 'You like football?'

'And beer,' I reply with a devilish smile.

He laughs a third time. Hopefully he's thinking about how interesting I am compared to the other women he knows.

'So why isn't your wife here?' I ask innocently. 'Is she at work?'

'No, she's, erm...' Peter pauses. And even though I know what he is going to say, I wait patiently to hear it.

'Karen's at her parents,' Peter tells me. 'She goes around to see them every few days. I'm not sure what time she'll be back though.'

He doesn't answer truthfully. He just makes up a white lie. That bodes well for the future, as well as explaining how he got away with doing things he shouldn't have in the past.

Peter has no reason to expect I know more, so I make sure not to show it.

I smile. 'That's nice. So it's just you and the kids? How's that going?'

'It's interesting.' Peter gives a weary smile back and then looks into the house again. It suggests that he's thinking about ending this conversation and getting back to the little people he is supposed to be looking after. But before he can say goodbye and close the door, I ask him another question.

'So I presume you like football and beer too?'

'Erm, yeah. I do.'

'Great! We should hang out sometime and watch a game. You could come to mine.'

Peter looks unsure about that. I sweeten the deal.

'Oh, I'm sorry. Your wife is welcome too, of course.' I

shrug as if she was an afterthought, which she is obviously intended to be.

'That's fine. Yeah, I'm sure we can all get together sometime,' he replies diplomatically. The sound of pattering feet in the hallway behind him interrupts us.

'Is Mummy home?' says a boy from inside the house. Then I get a glimpse of him on the other side of Peter.

'No, not yet. It's a new neighbour,' Peter tells his son, who I guess to be Oscar because I know he's the youngest. Having watched the family before, I know Noah is taller.

'Oh,' Oscar says, looking up at me with disappointment. He then turns and runs back down the hallway. Kids that age don't care about being rude. They just exist in their own little world.

They're lucky like that. Being an adult isn't as easy.

'Aww, he's cute,' I say with another smile.

'He can be,' Peter says. 'But he can also be a terror.'

I laugh, a little too hard, while reaching out and stroking his arm.

Peter looks awkward, but I can tell he enjoyed what I just did by the dilation of his pupils.

But then his stupid family responsibilities get the better of him.

'I should get back to them,' he says, thumbing behind him. All I hear are screaming noises and the sound of two boys running around.

'Of course. I'm sorry I kept you,' I say. 'It was a pleasure to meet you, and I hope I'll see you around.'

I end with another smile and more eye contact, and then I walk away, feeling pleased about how my first meeting with Peter went. As soon as I hear him close the front door, my fake smile disappears.

I'm glad that's over with; it's all just a means to an end. To him, I'm just a friendly, flirty woman who moved in around the corner.

But in reality, I'm the woman who is going to destroy his perfect little family.

By the time he realises, it will be too late.

14

KAREN

Peter's text message letting me know that everything was okay filled me with relief. I ordered a takeaway and ate it in the basement while watching a film. After, I went upstairs to bed, taking the book I started earlier with me.

Now I'm lying under a warm, thick duvet with the book in my hands and my head resting on a plump pillow. I feel as though I could nod off at any second. It's a far cry from how I usually feel at home, but I'm hoping that this 'reset' will make things easier for me when I do return.

Just before I drift off into a deep sleep, I hear my phone ringing. I grab it from the bedside table and see that Peter is calling me. I told him to give me a call once he got the kids into bed and had time to decompress. I guess he's done that. I answer the call.

'Hi, love,' I say, closing the book. I think I've done enough reading for one day. I want to save the rest of the story for tomorrow. 'Is everything okay?'

'Yeah, all good here,' Peter tells me, which sounds perfect, but I detect weariness in his voice.

'How are the boys?'

'Wild as always.'

'Are they in bed?'

'Yeah, they're asleep now.'

'Good. How was dinner?'

'A bit chaotic, but I managed it.'

'Well done. See, it's not as easy as I make it look.'

Peter laughs before agreeing.

'So how are things at the holiday home?' my husband wants to know. 'I hope it's a lot quieter than it is here.'

'Oh, Peter, it's wonderful,' I tell him. 'The house is beautiful, and the view is stunning.'

'What have you been doing?'

I update him on my activities so far, trying not to make it sound like I have been having too good a time. I know he has been stuck with more mundane tasks. But as I speak, I find it difficult to downplay my elation.

'Now I've just finished reading, and I'm going to sleep,' I tell him, wondering if he is also in bed. 'What about you?'

'I'm sitting on the sofa with a big glass of red wine. There's a game of football on the TV, and I'm not planning on moving for a while,' he admits. I laugh.

'So have there been any dramas tonight? Anything other than the usual, of course.'

Peter pauses before he answers. I presume it's because something is happening in the football match.

'Erm, no, it's been pretty standard,' he tells me. 'Nothing much to report.'

I guess that is a good thing, although not necessarily for this conversation because I sense it's going to peter out quickly without news from him. I don't know why, but I feel as though I need to keep my husband on the phone. Maybe it's because it might assuage a little of the guilt I'm feeling about abandoning him. Or maybe it's because I know we still have our issues, and running out of things to talk about is hardly going to help fix them.

'Do you miss me?' I ask him next, aware that it sounds a little needy, but hoping that he will indulge me.

'Yeah, of course I do,' he tells me matter-of-factly. It's a little less romantic than I had hoped. It also sounds like he is more interested in what is happening in the football game.

'Yeah, I miss you too,' I tell him, a little more sincerely than him, I hope. Then I hear commotion in the background.

'I've got to go. Oscar's stuck in the bathroom again,' Peter tells me.

I shake my head and smile. Everything is exactly the same even when I'm not there.

'Okay, goodnight, love,' I say and end the call. I put the phone down on the duvet beside the closed book with a sigh.

I'm not sure what I was expecting there, really. For him to beg me to come home? For him to tell me that he can't cope without me? Or that he might sound a little more convincing when telling me he misses me?

As I turn off the bedside lamp and snuggle under the duvet, I am acutely aware that escaping to here might only solve one of my two main problems. Yes, it will recharge my batteries, and that's a good thing. But putting distance between me and Peter will not solve the intimacy void in our marriage. Right then, I decide I'm going to have to be more aggressive on that front, even if I don't feel ready to be so.

That holiday he suggested? I'll tell him to book it. Just the two of us. We need to rediscover what we had. I feel as if we're just going through the motions of being husband and wife. We need to get back to what we were like before we had kids; otherwise I'm worried we're not going to last.

I don't want Peter to stray again, because I'm certain I won't be able to forgive him a second time. But I won't be able to forgive myself either if I don't do everything to make things better between us.

It shouldn't all be on him, even though he made the mistake. That's why I will return home with a new game plan, one that will hopefully bring us closer together.

But the more I think about it, the more I realise that I don't have to wait until I return to get started. What if I go home early? Spend tomorrow night in bed with my husband, where I belong?

I already feel much better after today. I still have all day tomorrow to unwind. But do I really need one more night away from Peter?

I decide to sleep on it and make my decision in the morning. I'll either stay for the full duration, or I will cut it short and go home to surprise my family. That would be a nice thing to do, to tell them how much I missed them and that I would rather be with them.

I'm sure they will be thrilled.

15

EVE

The sight of Karen sleeping as I watch her on my mobile phone interests me. But it's not the only person I can watch sleep tonight. All I have to do is look around the room I am in.

There's an overweight guy snoring away on his back. There's a skinny woman above him, curled up on her side, with her hands under her head. And there's an old man who keeps shifting in his sleep, pulling the bedsheet over before kicking it off again. These people are strangers, which makes it even weirder that I'm supposed to sleep here, but that's just how hostels and communal dorms work.

I'm here because Karen is staying where I usually do. Without much money, or family or friends to take me in, I have come here.

This hostel is in the centre of town, beside a busy street. I can hear the sounds of traffic through the single-glazed window that does little to keep the noise out, just as it does little to keep out the cold air.

There are six beds in here, consisting of three bunk beds. I am on the top of one because I was the last one to check in to this room, and all the bottom beds were gone. That meant I had to climb up the rickety ladder to get to my mattress, where I will try to sleep this evening.

Although, sleep seems unlikely in a place like this. Along with the sounds from outside, I have to deal with the snoring and fidgeting from the others. Not to mention the bright light that floods this room whenever someone decides to use the bathroom, waking everybody up in the process.

But hostels aren't exactly the place to be unselfish. Everybody is here for themselves. Tomorrow morning most of these people will leave, and new guests will check in. Places like this are not designed for long stays, and I'm glad I won't be here for a second longer than I have to be.

Checking my phone's screen, I see the reason I am here. I am sacrificing two nights of my life in this godforsaken place in exchange for my trickery of that woman. Having watched her for most of the day, she seems to be enjoying herself.

Takeaways. Books. Movies.

She's having quite the restful time. Now it looks like she is getting a restful night's sleep.

I hear a loud snort and glance over to see the overweight guy rolling onto his side. I hope the action will stop his snoring. But then it starts again.

I am suddenly jealous of Karen.

Letting out a sigh, I roll over, with my back to the room and facing the wall. I keep my phone active so I can watch Karen sleeping.

It's addictive to watch someone living their life while they have no idea someone is spying on them. It's not as if I can control Karen, dictate what she does next, but it is still fun to just watch. I learn a lot about a person from just watching.

When someone knows they are being watched, they will usually adapt their behaviour. Embarrassing habits are hidden away. Curious conduct is curtailed. Etiquette is flawless until they are alone again and can drop the pretence. That's when they might pick their nose or burp or scratch their bottom. It's when they might wipe off their makeup and go au naturel. And it's also when they are at their most vulnerable, not having to pretend like everything is okay when it isn't.

I observed Karen perform several embarrassing actions on camera today. I also saw her at her most honest – sitting on the sofa with no makeup on, wearing scruffy clothes, stuffing a slice of pizza into her mouth with no judgement. But she is being judged. I've been judging her from the second I heard about her, and I've certainly been judging her for every second I have been watching her on camera.

To me, she is not a real-life person but a character in a crazy TV show. I am not emotionally attached to her, because I know our relationship will end, like when a series reaches its conclusion. She is someone who exists for now, in my realm of consciousness, but soon she will cease to. And then I will move on with my life, as easily as a person changing channel.

I can't quite say the same about Peter though. My feelings run a little bit deeper where he is concerned.

I think back to our doorstep introduction earlier tonight. The way he leaned against the doorway, looking casual but also territorial, worried I might barge in. The way he laughed at my humorous quips, which showed me his fun side, confirming he liked me. And the way his eyes lit up for a moment when I mentioned us hanging out together. Drinking beer and watching football are two activities I have absolutely zero interest in, but he was intrigued.

There's no way he can deny the attraction. After a couple of minutes' interaction, I know I must already seem more interesting than Karen. That's precisely what I want him to think. I want him to think about me and about the possibility of seeing me again. Because he will see me again. Soon. And when he does, we will grow a lot closer.

I know a lot about Peter's interests, his routines, and his weakness around the opposite sex, but I learnt most of it from second-hand accounts. Now I'm very much looking forward to learning new things through our connection.

I can't wait to see him again.

I can't wait to get inside his home.

I can't wait to do it while Karen is enjoying herself in *my* home.

I turn off the feed and close my eyes, trying to get some sleep, so tomorrow comes that little bit quicker and I can get out of this hostel room. If I do manage to drift off, I hope to have a dream or two as well. Maybe I'll dream about Karen and Peter. Perhaps little Oscar might even make an appearance, like he did earlier. Or maybe I'll just have another nightmare about my late friend, because I've had plenty of them recently, and they are only getting worse.

I guess the only way I'll find out what awaits me is *to* sleep.

So I do.

When I wake, I feel happy, not because I failed to have a nightmare.

Because I'm another day closer to getting revenge.

16

KAREN

I stretch in the bed after what was easily the best night's sleep I've had in years. It's amazing how easy it is to get proper rest when there's nobody around to wake you up. No husband in the room getting ready for work. No kids running in and jumping on the bed, dying to tell me something, before racing out to cause chaos elsewhere. All I have are the sweet sounds of silence.

I check the time on my phone, surprised to see that it's 9am, which is further evidence of how peaceful my start to the day is.

It feels great to be waking up when I want, plodding to the bathroom that is all mine. The thoughts that enter my head are the ones I put there, and are not ones put there by one of the boys barging into my personal space. That's how I am able to think about pleasant things, like what's going to happen next in that book I am reading, or whether the sheep had as good a night's sleep as I did.

After brushing my teeth and making a cup of tea, I start my day.

I step outside and bask in the early morning sunlight

while admiring the special view that is right on my doorstep. I already know I'll miss these fields when I leave, so I'm making the most of them while I still have the chance.

After sleeping on my idea to cut my stay short, I decide to go ahead with that plan. One night was great, but two might just be too much. I'm sure Peter needs me at home, and I'm missing the kids like mad – more than I will miss this view – so I know that getting back to them sooner is the right thing to do. But I intend to use my last few hours here wisely. I head inside and get comfortable on the sofa. I continue the story I was reading last night.

My phone is next to me, because I am aware I should probably message Sarah soon and let her know the change of plans. I will stress to her that my decision has nothing to do with the wonderful holiday home and more to do with the fact that I'm missing my family too much. Sarah won't have a problem with that because I plan to pay her the full amount. I will make sure to leave this place in a respectable manner, so she has less cleaning up to do when she comes back here. I make a mental note to write a review before I go. I will be giving this place a glowing endorsement.

I'm making good progress with the book when I receive a text message. It's from Eve, and she is asking how my break is going so far.

I smile as I type my reply, glad she thought to check in with me. She really is a good friend, and I'm looking forward to seeing her again soon. I owe her one for telling me about this place. Perhaps I'll have her over to mine. I'll cook, and we can share a bottle of wine. She's never been to my house before, but it's about time I changed that. She can meet Peter, Noah and Oscar. But I won't ask her today. I'll mention it the next time I see her. For now, I let her know that I am having a wonderful time and that the view really is as special as she assured me it was.

I'm not expecting Eve to reply to me quickly – I know she will be busy working. So I'm surprised when she does. I read her message, and it seems like she has had a productive twenty-four hours too.

She's pleased to hear that I am enjoying my break before telling me that she has some exciting news of her own. She is going on a date tonight, and she wants me to wish her luck.

I waste no time in doing just that, aware of how momentous this is for Eve. She has been single for as long as I have known her – which is only two months – but in that time she hasn't mentioned going on dates before, so I assume it has been longer. It was getting to the point where I felt bad asking her for updates on her nonexistent love life. I'm pleased she is taking steps to remedy that now.

I reply: *How exciting! So who's the lucky guy? And where did you meet him?*

My enthusiasm might give away how much I've been waiting for this.

I close the book again, waiting for Eve's reply because, despite how enthralling the story is, it doesn't beat juicy gossip in the real world.

It takes Eve a little longer to get back to me, but when she does, she gives me a little more information about her potential new man.

I'm not telling you his name in case you go snooping on social media! But it's somebody I met recently, and we get on well enough, so we're seeing each other again.

I'm surprised by Eve's response. Not by the first part, because I would definitely go snooping if she gave me a name, but the second part is intriguing me because she sounds so casual about it. I tell her again that it all sounds very exciting, before asking for a report after on how the date went.

Eve promises me that she will. That seems like a good place to leave things.

I decide not to tell her about my plans. I'll let her think I'm still here while she is out on her date. But I genuinely can't wait to hear all about it after.

I should have asked what they plan to do. Dinner, drinks – a movie? Who knows?

It's been so long since I dated, I imagine the scene has changed a lot.

Whatever the plans, I hope it goes well. With a bit of luck, I might even get an introduction to this mystery man someday.

I just wonder who the lucky guy is.

17

EVE

I should probably stretch before I start jogging, or at least try to do something to avoid injury. I never was the most active and healthiest of people, preferring a rum over a run, and that probably explains why stretching feels unnatural to me. I joined the local gym so that I could befriend Karen, but throughout that time, I managed to get away with doing very little exercise. I mainly just walked around and chatted while everyone else got their sweat on. But I'm going to have to get my heart rate up a little bit now to make this next part of my plan seem convincing. So, with my hamstrings stretched as much as they can be, I put one foot in front of the other and run.

I've never understood the enjoyment of running on concrete, especially not in rainy weather. To me, it always looked like a dull way to spend time alone. And surely, it can't be good for the joints either? But I'm not planning on jogging for very long today. I just need to do it for long enough to make Peter and his kids think I was out for a while.

I can see the father and his two children up ahead, standing outside the school gates with all the other parents and pupils. Peter was on time today to collect his sons, unlike yesterday. That's good, because it means I required less time in the cold in my carefully assembled outfit to wait for him. It's not the right time of year to be outside in just a T-shirt and shorts, but that's what I am dressed in right now as I continue along at speed. The reason for wearing skimpy clothing instead of something warmer is so Peter sees me half naked. I want him to like what he sees when he does.

Despite my laziness, I have good legs and a nice body, and my legs are on full display now in these shorts, and a tight-fitting T-shirt does little to warm me up but shows off my breasts.

I hope Peter likes my outfit. He's about to see it in a couple of seconds.

Weaving my way through a few of the schoolkids who are walking away from the gates, I reach Peter, Noah and Oscar before they can make it to their car. And when I do, I act surprised to see my 'new neighbour' here.

'Peter! Hey!' I say, bringing a halt to my jog, in the spirit of being friendly.

Peter seems genuinely surprised to see me, as are his two sons, but I think on their part, it's because they don't know who I am. But their dad does.

'Oh, hi,' he says, not using my name like I used his. I wonder if it's because it has slipped his mind, or if he's too distracted by my outfit.

'How's it going?' I ask him, panting more to make it seem like I'm more out of breath than I am.

'Good, just collecting these two from school,' Peter replies, looking down at his sons, both of whom are eyeing me shyly.

'I see that. Did you have a good day at school, boys?'

My question draws a couple of nervous nods from the

youngsters before they look up at their father, possibly wondering who I am.

'You're brave going for a run in this weather dressed like that,' Peter says, nodding at my attire. 'Are you not cold?'

'I'm okay, but I've got to keep moving; otherwise I won't be able to feel my hands in a few minutes.'

'We'd better not hold you up, then,' he says with a smile, then opens the back door of his car.

The boys climb into the vehicle, but I linger. Before their father can join them in the warm interior, I hit him with a question.

'I was wondering, seeing how I've just bumped into you, how would you and your wife like to get together for a drink. Maybe tonight?'

Peter looks unsure, probably because I'm giving him very short notice.

'I can't do tonight, sorry,' he tells me. 'My wife is away, and I've got these two to look after.'

'Oh, of course. No problem. Another time?'

'Yeah, definitely.'

'Shall I take your phone number so I can text you?'

'Erm...' Peter hesitates.

He is likely still scarred from the last time he swapped numbers with a woman who was not his wife.

'Or I could just drop over when your wife is back?' I suggest. 'Maybe at the weekend?'

'Yeah, that would be best,' Peter tells me, relieved that I'm giving him another option that doesn't involve swapping digits with an attractive woman. A woman whom his kids might mention when their mum returns home tomorrow.

'Great! Well, hopefully, I'll see you around!' I say breezily. 'Have a fun night tonight looking after your boys!'

With that, I give Peter and the boys peering out of the car

a quick wave before I turn and jog away. Dodging children in uniform, I make it to the corner.

Once out of sight, I stop pretending to be some kind of fitness freak. My lungs are on fire. I put my hands on my hips. I'm absolutely freezing and in desperate need of a hot shower. But at least my efforts were worth it. Not only did I see Peter and give him a glimpse of what I look like under a winter coat and scarf, but I also confirmed he will be at home tonight, looking after the boys.

That's good, because I intend to see him again this evening.

It would have been nice if he invited me around to his tonight while he looks after the boys, but it doesn't matter. I'm going to make it happen anyway. I'm going to turn up on his doorstep, and he is going to let me inside. That's because one, I'm persuasive, and two, he is weak. Then once I'm in the house, I can carry out the next part of my plan while Karen sits in the holiday home with no idea as to what her husband is up to.

For a man who has already been caught cheating once, it won't look good when new photographic evidence turns up of him with another woman in his home, particularly if he and the woman were in a state of undress in those photos. But that's exactly what is going to happen after I pay him a visit tonight.

There will be evidence pointing to him being unfaithful again.

And it will be more than enough to blow up his marriage for a second time – except this time, the damage will be irreparable.

I'm sure Peter is thinking that the worst thing to happen would be for his wife to leave him and take the kids. But he has no idea that worse will be waiting for him if he isn't careful.

Everything is going well so far. I didn't even pull my hamstring during my short jog, so I guess the stretching paid off. I rush back to that grimy hostel, eager to get out of the cold and get some feeling back in my arms and legs.

I certainly haven't missed being away from the hostel. I rush through the small reception area, grab a towel from my bed and go into one of the shower rooms. As I wait for the water in the shower to warm up, I make a quick check on my phone, to see how Karen is getting on, and see her curled up on the sofa, reading a book. That all seems pretty normal, so I leave my phone on my clothes, get into the shower and relax as the hot water does its job. After, I return to the shared bedroom and lie down on the bed. The other occupants are out at present, giving me a chance to catch up on some of the sleep I lost out on last night. Feeling sleepy and warm, I also feel good about how things are going.

Being cold today was worth it, because I know Peter will have been thinking about me as he drove his sons home. How could he not? He wouldn't have been thinking about his wife, that's for sure, and the same will go for later tonight.

It turns out that I should have set an alarm, because I ended up sleeping a little longer than I wanted. I am woken by one of my roommates making noise by their bunk bed, but they actually did me a favour this time, because I need to see Peter.

Despite that little setback, I'm out of the hostel in good time and on my way to his home. I even checked on Karen before I left. As usual, nothing concerned me. She was sitting in the movie room, watching the news.

How exciting.

I expect that I will have a better night than her.

And I expect that Peter will too.

18

After last night's debacle with the oven, I decided not to cook tonight. So it's a trip to the local chip shop instead. Karen told me that she didn't want the boys eating takeaways while she was gone, but a bag of chips is hardly the worst thing. Besides, if the boys keep the secret, then their mum never has to find out about it.

Both Noah and Oscar were happy to enter that pact. I suspect it might have been because neither of them could bear another night of me faffing around in the kitchen, but I got them on side easily enough. The empty chip wrappers on the table prove how popular tonight's meal was. Now that one more potential headache is out of the way, all that's left is to get the boys upstairs to bed.

'When is Mum coming home?' Noah asks me as we climb the staircase. The third time since Karen left.

'Tomorrow, like I said,' I reply.

'I still don't understand why she has gone away.'

'I told you. She's busy, but she will be back soon, and then she won't be going away again.'

I'm not quite sure if that last part is true, but I say it

anyway, to make my eldest son feel better. It makes me feel a little better too. Having this alone time with the kids has given me a little glimpse into what things would have been like if Karen and I had split. Not only would we have had to split financial assets but also custody. Most likely, I would have to make do with spending one or two weekends with them a month, at most.

The thought of only being able to see Noah and Oscar at agreed times rather than whenever is more frightening than having to look after myself for a whole weekend, because, as these last few days have proven, it's not easy. Karen has the patience of a saint, and her forgiveness will always be something that I am forever grateful for. I just wish she were home now. But she isn't, so I've got another fun evening alone ahead.

In the next half an hour Noah manages to do most of what I ask of him, but it's a different story for Oscar. He is running around the upper part of the house, as if he is being chased by an invisible monster.

'What are you doing? I told you it's time for bed!' I say with all the exasperation of a parent who still remembers what life was like when the evenings were spent doing something fun instead of something painstaking.

'I'm busy!' Oscar tells me as he races past me again before firing one of his toy guns at the corner of the room, as if he really needs to shoot something there.

I love that my youngest has a vivid imagination, and I'm also a little jealous that he can still entertain himself with nothing but what's in his mind. I passed that point a long time ago, but I would love him a lot more if he just got in his bed, like his brother did.

It takes more wasted minutes and a load of effort before I get Oscar to do what I ask. By the time I turn the lights out in their bedroom and wish them a goodnight, I feel ready to collapse into my own bed. It's only 8pm, but I'm seriously tempted to have an early night myself. I also like the fact that when I wake up, it will only be a couple of hours before Karen returns home.

But plans for an early night are put on hold when I hear a knock on the front door.

I wince, worried the sound will cause the boys to get out of their beds and investigate. But their bedroom doors remain closed, and there's no sound from them. I waste no time going downstairs before another knock might wake them. I open the door, surprised to see my new neighbour standing on the doorstep, holding a bottle of wine.

'Natasha?'

'Hey, Peter! How are you?'

'Erm, good. Can I help you?'

'Yeah, I was thinking about what you said earlier when we saw each other at the school. About how you were looking after your kids while your wife was away. I thought you might want a little company. It seems silly for me to be on my own around the corner while you're stuck in, so how about a little drink?'

Natasha holds up the bottle of wine, although that's not the only thing that gets my attention. I catch sight of her bare legs flashing from beneath the trendy coat she is wearing. While she is dressed a little better for the weather than she was earlier, she still has a surprising amount of skin on show.

'What do you say?' she asks me after I fail to answer her. 'Let's have a drink and a chat. I hope you aren't going to turn me away, or I might have to go knocking on another neighbour's door for company instead.'

It's the surprise of seeing her turn up on my doorstep mixed in with the possibility she will make me feel guilty if I reject her friendliness that has me stepping aside. I allow her in, but not before I tell her to be quiet because the kids are in bed.

She enters my home, and I do a check of the dark street before I close the door. It's almost an involuntary thing for me to do. I worry my wife is out there in the shadows watching me, preparing to catch me up to no good with another woman again. But of course she isn't out there, and of course I'm not going to do anything I shouldn't with Natasha. I'll just be friendly. Natasha is obviously lonely, and she seems to have latched onto me a little. I assume it's because she doesn't know anybody else around here. It's also possible the other neighbours she spoke to weren't as friendly as me.

But she is in my house. I must be on guard.

Make small talk. Have a glass of wine. And then politely ask her to leave, because I am a family man and I have family responsibilities.

Then I see Natasha take off her coat and hang it on the banister, as if she is already making herself at home. The dress she is wearing is flowery and fitted. I guess it's still quite a casual look, but there's nothing casual about my observation of her. I'm already regretting letting her in.

How the hell would I explain another woman in the house to Karen if she came home right now?

I guess I'm lucky that she won't be.

19

KAREN

I finished the book I started only yesterday, delighted by how the plot unfolded, before wrapping up with a satisfactory conclusion. As I often do, I promise myself that I won't leave it too long until I start another one, but that's always easier said than done. Life's responsibilities tend to get in the way of many things, and reading time is one of them.

It's being aware of all those responsibilities that made me pack up my things in the late afternoon, making good on my decision to leave earlier than planned. It didn't take me long to get my belongings back in my suitcase. If Peter were here, he would have been happy to tell me I overpacked. He's right, of course. I barely used half the items I brought, but it's always better to take too much than not enough.

With my suitcase sitting by the front door, I found myself lingering a little longer, almost as if I was savouring my last chance to enjoy some 'me time' before going home. I made myself a cup of tea, finished off the chocolates that somehow survived without me devouring them, and watched the local news on the TV in the basement.

There wasn't much to report on – very little of note

happens in this region – but I was still entertained by the news bulletin. Clearly, the novelty of watching TV on a huge screen hasn't worn off yet. If Peter or the boys were here and saw the size of this TV, they would be begging me to get one. I dread to think how much a TV this size costs. But they aren't here, so only I will know how cool it is to sit in front of one.

But as the clock neared eight, I figured I should probably make a move, catch the kids before they go to bed. I went upstairs with the intention of calling a taxi, then waiting by the door for it to arrive. But then I remembered I wanted to leave a review for Sarah, so I took a seat at the table and picked up the pen that was tucked inside the book.

And that's where I still am now, because I'm struggling with what to write.

I don't want to give some boring, generic review, like most of the other ones in this book. I want to be different for, one, originality and, two, because I really do think this place is great. I want that to come across when Sarah checks this book tomorrow. That's why I'm taking my time with it. I'm hoping I'll get a boost of creativity, maybe add something a little witty in my review, so future guests might enjoy it too. But my talents don't lie with a pen, and in the end, I just leave the review I should have written ten minutes ago.

This is a truly wonderful holiday home, and I enjoyed every second of my stay. Thank you for having me here, Sarah, and I will be sure to come back again and again! P.S. the champagne and chocolates were a lovely touch and were very much enjoyed! Xx

With the review written, I close the book and walk to the front door, where my suitcase is waiting for me. Each step closer to that door makes me excited to be seeing my children soon, and I'm also looking forward to some time with Peter.

Even though this has only been a short stay, I feel as if things are going to be so much better now.

My only regret, as I wait by the door for the taxi to arrive, is that I didn't get to meet Sarah in person. It would have been nice to chat with her, find out a little more about her, rather than just speaking over email. But maybe she used to do things in a more personal way. Maybe it got too time consuming for her, so she changed her method of doing business. I can see how having to make the same small talk with every single guest could get a little boring after a while. Still, I wish I had met her. I don't even know what she looks like, or how old she is, or what she gets up to while someone is staying here. But I guess none of that really matters. I see the taxi arrive outside, and I prepare to leave the house, making sure to put the key in the lockbox before I depart.

I discover that the taxi driver is not one for small talk either as he drives me closer to town. But that just gives me time to check my phone and catch up on a few messages, most of which I have not read. I didn't want to get caught up doing normal things. But I reply to all the messages now because I'm on my way back to reality. But it's as I am doing so, I see the last message from Eve that she sent me earlier. She was one of the few people whom I interrupted my personal time to reply to, and I remember that she is on her date tonight. I don't want to interrupt it, but sending another quick good luck message won't do any harm.

The taxi rolls through the centre of town while I message Eve. I look out the window at the various bars and restaurants lining the high street. I wonder if Eve is in one of these venues now, being wined and dined by her potential new boyfriend. It's possible, but wherever she is, I hope she is enjoying herself.

I spend the rest of the journey wondering what kind of reception I will receive when I arrive home. I expect Noah and Oscar will be excited to see me returning early and greet me with a hug, because that's generally how they greet any family member they haven't seen in more than twenty-four hours. They might also be thrilled to have me back for dinners. I'm guessing the food was less than desirable over the past two nights, thanks to their father's lack of culinary skills.

But it's Peter's possible reaction to seeing me home early that intrigues me the most. It will be yet another test of where we stand at present. If his reaction to seeing me is just as warm, then I'll know that he really did miss me and loves having me back. But if he's a little aloof, or even just a little unsure, then it will be another sign that we still have a problem.

I'm nervous as the taxi turns onto our street, which seems silly because it's home, but that's just how I feel.

I don't know it yet, but in a couple of minutes, I won't be the only one feeling that way.

20

It was as easy as I thought it would be to get into Peter and Karen's house. As I suspected, Peter can't turn away a pretty woman on his doorstep, and certainly not one with her legs on show and a bottle of wine in her hand. Now the two of us are sitting in the living room, and while we are on different sofas, I plan on closing that distance during the evening.

Peter keeps mentioning how tired he is, how he can only have one drink because he has to be up early in the morning. But I'm confident I can change his mind. It's all excuses; he's uncomfortable about being alone with an attractive woman, and why wouldn't he be? He's been a naughty boy before. The last thing he wants is to make his wife worry that it might have happened again.

'You have such a lovely home,' I say as I look around the room. In reality, the décor is not to my taste, and it's certainly not as nicely decorated as the house Karen is currently in. I'm just being polite.

'Thanks. It's mostly down to my wife. She makes all the decisions when it comes to interior design.'

'I'm sure you gave a helping hand.'

'Not really. I did a bit of painting and put a shelf up. But I was working under strict instructions while I did it.'

I laugh and run the tip of my finger around the rim of my glass, eyes on the task. When I look up, I see that Peter is watching it too.

'It's a little odd how I've met you three times now, yet I still haven't met your wife,' I say after a brief lull in the conversation. 'Where did you say she was again?'

'Er, she's busy. Family. Work. She's got a lot going on at the minute. But she'll be back at some point tonight.'

Peter's lies amuse me, because he has no idea how much I know about where his wife is. The way he is able to do it so easily hints at how easily he must have deceived Karen during his affair.

But he can't deceive me.

'Is that why you're on edge?' I ask him. 'You're worried about her coming back and finding me here?'

'I'm not on edge,' Peter says defensively.

'Oh, I'm sorry. I just…you seem a bit nervous.'

I make a point of crossing my legs, to draw his eyes from mine and down to my bare skin.

'No, not at all,' he says before taking a glug of his wine. 'Like I said, I'm just tired. It's been a long week, and looking after two boys makes it feel a lot longer.'

'Yeah, I can't imagine how hard it must be having two little ones to look after. I'm not sure I'll ever be ready for children of my own.'

'They're not all bad. But it is hard work, I'm not going to lie.'

'Yeah, that's what I hear. I guess I'll be ready to think about them one day. But for now, I just want to enjoy myself. No commitment, no responsibility, you know what I mean?'

I smile at Peter and pause, allowing my last few words to

linger in the air. Here is a man who is drowning in commitment and responsibility, and here I am making sure he knows that I am not.

I wait for him to break the silence, and when he does, he makes an excuse that he needs to go to the toilet.

I make sure to smile as he leaves the room. The second he's gone, I shoot forward and put my wine glass down on the coffee table. Then I quickly scurry into the hallway and get my phone out of my coat pocket that's hanging up, before racing back to the living room and taking a few select photos.

The first photo is of my red fingernails resting on the frame of a hanging picture with the four smiling family members who live here. The second photo is of the two half-full glasses on the table beside the bottle of wine. And then the third is a picture of my feet resting on the coffee table, my bare legs on show, making it look like I am very much at home.

With the images captured on my phone, I'm about to put it away when I stop. I decide to make a quick check on Karen before Peter returns. Opening the app that allows me to see the hidden camera footage at the house, I flick between cameras in my search for her. But she's not in the living room, nor is she in the kitchen or bathroom. She isn't in the basement either, so that must mean she is in the bedroom. Perhaps she has had an early night.

But when I see that she isn't in there either, I begin to worry.

'Where the hell are you?' I mutter as I frantically flick between all the cameras, wondering how I managed to miss her. But I can't see her anywhere, and it's only when I go back to the kitchen camera that I realise what has happened.

Not only is the kitchen tidy, but the review book on the table is sitting open. That suggests to me that Karen has arranged it like that so the owner will see it when she next visits.

That must mean she has left a review.

And that must mean she has left the house.

I can't believe it. Karen has cut short her stay.

Why has she done that?

More importantly, where is she now?

I'm aware that her coming home and catching me here would ruin my plan, because Peter could talk his way out of it. And without any saucier photos than me with my feet on the coffee table, Karen might buy it. But if I can control this situation, then I can control the narrative, and right now I'm not in control.

If Karen is on her way home, I need to get going. There's no way for me to know that for sure, but I have to err on the side of caution. That's why I plan to tell Peter that I have to go when he comes back down. But as I wait for him, I see several flashes appear on his mobile phone that he left on the arm of the sofa.

Intrigued by how many he is getting all of a sudden, I pick up the phone to check on them.

That's when I see he has a missed call and a new text message from Karen.

I'm outside in a taxi, but I don't have any cash for the driver. Could you bring some out? xx

Karen is outside the house? My heart races as I look towards the window.

I'm grateful that the curtains are drawn; otherwise she would likely see me standing in here. But just because she hasn't caught me yet doesn't mean she won't in a moment's time.

The sound of Peter coming back down the stairs sends me

rushing out into the hallway. I hand him his phone, then tell him that I think his wife is back.

His mouth drops open when he hears the news. His mood doesn't improve when he reads the text message on his phone.

'You need to go,' he tells me before I have a chance to say anything else. 'Please. I'm sorry, but you need to leave right now.'

'Erm, okay,' I say, pretending like this is a surprise to me, but secretly pleased because I need out of this house as desperately as Peter does.

'The back door,' he tells me as he hands me my coat. I follow him in silence through the kitchen and towards the door that will give me my escape route.

'Is everything okay?' I ask him as he unlocks the door and checks outside, likely confirming that it is safe for me to go out that way.

'Yeah, fine. I'm sorry. You can get out down the side of the house. But if you could wait until my wife has gone inside, I would appreciate it.'

'Er, yeah. Sure.'

It's at that point that Peter practically pushes me out of the door, and while it's not particularly forceful, it's another sign of how desperate he is to not get caught with another woman.

As I hear the back door close and lock behind me, I look around at the dark garden that I'm now forced to lurk in until I know Karen is inside the house. I can make out the faint outline of a shed, as well as a table and chair set that probably gets a lot of use in the summer months. But I don't waste any more time hanging around back here. Instead, I creep down the side of the property.

I feel like I'm doing a good job of staying quiet and hidden, or at least I was until my foot knocks into something.

The loud cracking sound a second later has me holding my position and fearing the worst.

Did Karen hear me from the front of the house? It's possible, so I stay as still as I can until a few more seconds pass and I feel confident nobody is coming around here to check.

Reaching the corner of the house, I peep around it. When I do, I see Karen walking up the driveway towards her front door. Peter is beside her, presumably having run out to pay the taxi driver. He is carrying his wife's suitcase.

What a gentleman.

Karen has no idea that he just kicked a woman out of his house.

Peter is a man of many surprises. But, as I'm beginning to realise, so is Karen.

She left the holiday home early.

I need to find out why.

I also need to make sure I don't let this little hiccup steer me off my intended course.

But as I stand there, beside the house of the man whose selfish actions contributed to the death of my best friend, I feel a rage inside me. It burns even more intensely than I anticipated. I came here to sow the seeds that would put an end to Peter and Karen's relationship for good. But after being around him, seeing how unaffected he is by Leanne's death, I suddenly feel like I'm not doing enough to mess with him.

Peter taught me how painful it is to lose someone I love; maybe it's only fair that I teach him the same thing.

Instead of just ending his marriage, I should just end his life.

But not yet. Not before he experiences the same anguish as me, the anguish of seeing someone he loves die.

21

PETER

My heart is still racing as I close the front door and put Karen's suitcase down. Even though I know that Natasha is out of the house now, I still feel as though my wife is going to find out what I have been up to while she was away, even though I technically did nothing wrong.

It was only an innocent chat on a sofa over a bottle of a wine.

The wine.

I realise that the bottle and two glasses are still on the coffee table in the living room. If Karen sees it, she will have questions. I was supposed to be the only grown-up in the house. Why would two glasses be out?

I need to make sure she doesn't go into that room before I have a chance to tidy up. But as well as that, I'm also curious to know why my wife came back earlier than expected.

'This is a surprise,' I say, being honest. If only Karen knew how much. 'What happened?'

'Nothing, I was just missing you all.' Karen takes off her

coat and hangs it on the banister, where another woman's coat was moments ago. 'That's okay, isn't it?'

'Yeah, of course. It's just if I had known, I could have picked you up.'

'That's okay. I'm back now. Are the kids in bed?'

'Yeah, I managed to get them up a bit earlier than usual.'

'How did you manage that?'

'Mainly through bribery and witchcraft.'

Karen laughs at my joke, and I wish I could be as relaxed as she seems to be after her time away, but I still need to get that second wine glass out of the living room before she walks in there.

'I won't go up and wake them, then,' my wife says, turning towards the living room door. 'But I wouldn't say no to a cup of tea if you're making one.'

'Yeah, sure!' I say, blocking the living room door so she can't go through it. 'How about you get your pyjamas on while I put the kettle on, and then you can tell me all about your trip.'

Karen thinks about my suggestion for a moment before agreeing that it would be nice to get more comfortable. To my relief, she heads for the staircase while I pretend to go into the kitchen. But I change course as soon as she is out of view, and rush into the living room, where I scoop up the incriminating evidence. I'll get rid of it by putting the glasses in the dishwasher and hide the bottle somewhere before Karen comes back downstairs.

By the time the kettle has boiled and I have made us each a cup of tea, Karen is back, wearing her pyjamas. We sit beside each other on one sofa, and I ask her for the full report on her break.

But while she runs through a list of activities that range from reading, watching films and scoffing chocolates, I'm only half-listening. I'm distracted by Natasha. What must she be thinking after I kicked her out of this house so abruptly? I wonder what she made of my overreaction to my wife coming home early.

From her point of view, there was no reason why she couldn't have stayed, sipping wine on my sofa. I could have introduced Karen to her, and the three of us could have continued the conversation. But acting as if Natasha being here would be a disaster for my marriage must have come across as a strange way to behave. I should explain myself to our new neighbour at a later date.

But the problem is I don't want to explain myself, because doing so would be admitting to her that I was unfaithful once. Not only would that make me look bad, but it might also give Natasha ideas.

I know she has been flirting with me, and I know she deliberately wore a revealing dress tonight. As much as she plays the friendly, lonely neighbour, I know it's not normal for a woman to just show up at a guy's house with a bottle of wine when she knows his wife is away, and invite herself in. That's not being neighbourly. That's being seductive.

I would prefer it if Natasha went on presuming that I am a faithful husband who wouldn't be interested if she tried to make a move on me. But how else can I explain pushing her out the back door while my wife comes in the front one?

With a bit of luck I won't see Natasha again, and that will eliminate the need for any explanation. I'd like to think she won't turn up here again unannounced, and I'd like to think that I won't bump into her outside the school gates now that Karen is back on duty.

Maybe this is the end of our brief relationship. I hope so. I need to focus on my wife, not the flirty neighbour, who almost certainly would have suggested a second glass of wine.

'And then I flew around the house on a great, big, fire-breathing dragon!'

I frown as I try to process what Karen just said to me.

After a few seconds of confusion, 'What?' is all I can muster.

'Oh, so you *are* listening to me?' she asks, and that's when I realise that it's obvious my mind was wandering.

'Sorry, love, I was listening,' I say, fearing we might be on the verge of another argument. It doesn't look good that after not seeing my wife for two days, I can barely spare two minutes to listen to her.

Thankfully, Karen does not seem too annoyed by my mistake.

'Never mind. I guess it's not much fun listening to me tell you about all the fun things I've been up to while you've been juggling work and the kids.'

'It hasn't been that bad, honestly,' I say with a grin, but Karen isn't buying it. She smiles knowingly.

'Thanks for letting me go away, Peter. I know it can't have been easy, but it was just what I needed. And I promise I won't do it again. The next time I have a holiday, you're coming with me.'

'That would be wonderful.'

I take a sip of my tea, but it does not taste as nice as the drink I was enjoying before Karen came home. But at least my heart has stopped racing now, and as we continue to chat, I feel confident that I got away with what happened tonight. But that doesn't mean I'm not annoyed at myself for getting into another situation that could cause problems in my marriage. There's no need for me to be doing anything to give Karen reason to be paranoid. I don't want to make the same mistake again. I don't need another woman in this house, even if it was intended as a friendly gesture to someone looking for a little company. All I need to do is make sure

Karen and the kids are looked after. That's it. Natasha can look after herself.

I'm about to suggest we put the TV on and watch an episode of one of the shows we recorded when Karen says she fancies an early night. She follows with a wink, and it's clear what she is really in the mood for. I happily put the remote control down on the arm of the sofa and follow her upstairs.

As I'm kissing my wife on the bed where I spent last night alone, I can tell the time away has done wonders for Karen and her mood. She's rarely been affectionate with me since my affair. Hopefully, this means we have turned the corner, and things will get better from here.

Is that too much to ask for?

22

KAREN

Reality is biting hard on my first day back in the real world.

After arriving home early to surprise Peter, and after a rare but enjoyable 'early night' with him, I was feeling well rested and relaxed as the sun rose over town this morning. But that changed the second Noah and Oscar came bounding into the bedroom. While it is brilliant to see them again, it is a reminder that my life has shifted suddenly from the slow lane back into the fast lane.

After making breakfast for the boys and dropping them off at school, I make it to my desk with a minute to spare, saving me from another glaring look from my manager. I begin by sifting through all the emails that have built up in my inbox while I was off.

The morning drags, as it usually does, so different to the one morning I spent at that lovely house. That book I read? I'm still thinking about it now. I really must see if the author has written anything else, but I'm not quite sure when I'll get time to read it.

Midday signals the beginning of my lunch hour, that

sixty-minute beacon of hope in the middle of the slog to the 3pm finish line, when I can abandon my duties and rush over to the local school to get the kids. I sit in the staff room and make small talk with a couple of my colleagues, who are interested in hearing about my break and ask me if I could bring in the leaflet so they can take a look. I promise I will do just that while hoping that I still have the leaflet at home. I don't remember throwing it out, so it should still be around. I'm sure I'll come across it when I'm tidying up after the boys later tonight.

The arrival of the manager into the staff room cuts short any gossip about the 'idiots who run this place'. I take the cue as a good time to return to my desk and crack on with the afternoon. I am looking forward to the clock striking three so I can collect Noah and Oscar and hear all about their day. Before I reach that point, I receive a text message from Sarah.

Hi Karen. Just wanted to thank you for the lovely review you left. It was very kind. I'm glad you enjoyed your stay, and you are more than welcome again in the future, if you feel like you need another break!

I smile at her pleasant message before typing out my response, making sure that my manager isn't watching me as I do.

Thank you, Sarah. It really was brilliant and was just what I needed! I'm not sure I can cope with leaving my family behind again to go on holiday on my own, but I have a couple of work colleagues who are interested in booking a stay, so hopefully I can get you a little more custom!

I send the message, feeling satisfied with my response, because even though I'm unlikely to be booking again, I might be able to send a few more guests her way. Sarah said word of mouth was her main way of advertising, so I imagine she will be more than happy to hear that. Sure enough, her response is a positive one.

That's great. Much appreciated. Just to let you know, I run a monthly competition for all the guests who have stayed with me before. You all get entered in the draw, and one lucky guest wins a free night. Would you like me to enter you in it? You could bring your partner if you win.

I think about the competition for a few seconds, but can't find a reason not to say yes. I would love the chance of winning a free stay at that holiday home, especially if I can take Peter with me.

Wow, yes, please. I never win anything, but happy to have a go! Thank you!

I'm not exaggerating when I say to Sarah that I never win anything, because I genuinely don't. I've had no luck when it comes to competitions, and it's been that way forever. Even as a child, some of my friends would win competitions at school or in the local newspaper. I was always the one who participated but never got the prize. I guess that explains why I very rarely play prize games now, including the lottery. Yes, I'm aware that by never entering I am even less likely to win, turning my bad luck into a self-fulfilling prophecy. But I'm happy to participate in this competition, and who knows, maybe my luck will start to turn soon.

Sarah messages me back to confirm that I am now entered; then she wishes me good luck and a good day. I put my phone away before my boss catches me using it, and do more work. Excitement builds as I work, because being in a draw means there is a chance I could get some good news soon. It doesn't really matter if I don't win the free night at the holiday home. The one night I already had there was good enough for me. There must be lots of guests in that draw. I wonder what my odds are of winning.

Slim to none, most likely.

While I might not be fortunate enough to win a competition, I am fortunate enough to see the digital clock on my computer screen tick over to 15:00. That means I can leave. I say goodbye to the pair I spoke to in the kitchen, telling them I will try to remember to bring in that leaflet tomorrow. But maybe I shouldn't be in such a rush to do that, because I'd only be decreasing my chances of winning the competition, wouldn't I?

THE DRIVE over to the school is a slightly less stressful experience than usual; I catch a few more green lights than red ones. By the time my boys are in the back seat and telling me about their day, I am smiling and happy because as exhausting as it is to be a parent, it's good to be back in my familiar routine. I'm not sure what I would do without Peter, Noah and Oscar to keep me busy all the time. I was feeling a little guilty about leaving the three of them behind. I feel another tug on my heartstrings when Oscar makes me promise him that I won't ever go away again.

I assure my son that I am not, and he seems satisfied with that answer, because he goes back to shoving crisps into his mouth and staring out the window. I also notice a little smile on Noah's face when he hears the same news. Then he makes me laugh by saying he is glad about that because Daddy is a rubbish cook and not as good as Mummy is. I have to agree with him there. Noah launches into an entertaining recount of Peter's attempts to make fish fingers, chips and beans. By the time we make it home, my cheeks are hurting from all my smiling.

I slip into parent mode to make sure the boys get into the house without running off and onto the busy road outside our home. Just before I head inside, I glance down the street because I thought I saw someone watching me.

I only got a brief glimpse of them, and it wasn't long enough to recognise them before they ducked behind a hedge. I think it was a woman with a woolly bobble hat. She was wearing sunglasses, so I couldn't identify her.

I'm not sure what she was doing, whoever she was, but when I look around, she seems to have gone.

I head inside and forget about her.

23

EVE

I've allowed a week to pass since Sarah messaged Karen about the 'competition'. Of course, there is no competition. With Karen as my only guest, it's a guarantee that it will be her name drawn out of the hat. I'm going to message her again today and let her know she won. I expect her to return to this house and bring Peter with her. After having planted the seed already, I expect this next part of my plan to go smoothly.

But having to wait a week to implement it has been frustrating, even though I know patience is key to this plan working. Going too fast will only raise suspicions on Karen's part. She needs to think that other people have been staying at the holiday home since she left it. She also needs to think that it took me a little time to sort out this competition.

So far, I am playing it all just right.

The message, in which I will tell Karen she is the winner, is already written and ready to be sent on my mobile, but I haven't pressed send just yet. I am hoping to see Karen's reaction when she receives it. I plan to do that by returning to the school, where I know she will be collecting her kids. Now, watching from a safe distance as she gets out of her car, I have her well and truly in my sights.

My target chats with a couple of the other mums who are waiting at the gates; it all looks friendly and familiar. I wonder if Karen is genuine friends with any of the parents. The way she so easily engages in conversation with two other women suggests they are already pals. The sight of her chatting and smiling with them only frustrates me.

I guess it's because I lost the only real friend I had in this world, so I don't care to see Karen interacting with her own social circle.

I wonder what they are talking about. Maybe it's something 'hilarious' that one of their children did recently. Perhaps it is about an upcoming parents evening, or some insignificant change in how the school does something that warrants a deep discussion. Or it could be that they are planning their next get-together, a girls' night, complete with all the nonsense talk that such a plan demands.

Whatever it is, I despise the fact that Karen seems to have many options when it comes to friends and activities. Unlike me. I lost my one and only true friend.

If I didn't hate Karen so much, then I suppose we could actually be friends – real ones – instead of the fake friends we are at present. As far as she knows, I am just like all her other pals, but she is so wrong. I am nothing like them, all wittering away with too much makeup plastered on their faces as they wait for their children to finish school so they can go home to their perfect little lives. I don't talk to Karen because I want to feel good about myself, or because we have something in common, or because I love to talk about myself – like I imagine all these women here do.

I am only in her life for one plain and simple reason.

To end it.

Taking out my phone, I decide that now is a good time to

send the message. As it flies through the ether from my device to hers, I wait eagerly for her to check her mobile and see the good news. But annoyingly, she is too busy chatting to notice, forcing me to wait a little longer.

As I stand there on the street corner, a little more hidden than when Karen almost caught me peeping out from behind a hedge near her house, I notice a new message come through. It's from someone called Kim. In the text, she tells me that she heard about the holiday home from her work colleague Karen and is interested in booking a stay.

I roll my eyes, because this is the second such message I received in the last couple of days. The first one was also from a work colleague of Karen's. She obviously told them about the holiday home and how they must go and book a stay too. In fairness, Karen did tell me she would pass on my details, but I thought she might forget.

I wonder if she showed them the leaflet I made especially for her. Probably, but it doesn't matter. All I need to do is reply to this message the same way as the first one and tell Karen's work friend that there is not much availability over the next few weeks, but I will let her know when things quieten down. Then there are those interested in buying the house. I know I won't be able to put off prospective clients forever without making them suspicious, but I don't need to. I'm close to finishing what I started with Karen and Peter. After, the house will be available to anybody who wants to buy it.

Although by the time I finish, I think it will be the last place anybody wants to go.

I'll reply to Kim later, whenever I'm bothered, but for now, I go back to watching Karen. The gates open and the kids run out, like they do every time, desperate to get home and forget about maths, English and science for another day. I watch her face light up when she sees Noah and Oscar, and as she leads her sons to her parked car, I worry that she isn't going to look at her phone. But just before she gets in, she checks her device. The little pause she gives before getting in her car tells me my message has been received.

Then I see her typing, and I wonder if she is going to respond to me right now.

The vibration on my phone a second later gives me my answer. I look down to see what Karen said.

Oh my gosh! Are you serious? I never win anything! I can't believe it! Thank you.

Wow, she really is excited to be the winner of a competition with only one entrant. Bless her. That just means she will be even more disappointed when she finds out the truth. But for now, I will let her bask in the glow of her 'victory'. I reply to confirm that she has indeed won, and mention again that she should let me know when she and her husband would like to stay.

After sending that message, I watch Karen some more, but she doesn't reply. Instead, she gets in her car and drives home, because she is a busy woman and she doesn't have time to stand around on the street all day texting. Unlike me.

Now that Karen has gone and I've done what I need to do for today, I'm at a loose end again. I guess I'll just go back to the house and bide my time until Karen tells me when she wants to stay again. It is lonely in that house all by myself, but at least I'm not going back to the hostel.

I watch the other mums departing the school with their kids in tow, seeing how full their lives are. They aren't alone, and they certainly don't have time to kill in between all the tasks on their to-do lists.

They aren't feeling as empty as I am.

They haven't lost something they can never get back.

24

EVE

ONE YEAR AGO

I knock on Leanne's door, excited to see my friend and spend a fun evening with her. Her house really is beautiful, and it's one of the reasons why I'm happy to take her up on her invite to come over. It's better than going out in town or, worse, back to the poxy flat I'm living in at present.

'Hi, babe! Come in!' Leanne says with her usual energy as she opens the door. I'm armed with the things I always bring when we are having a girly night in. The essentials consist of wine, chocolates, and a couple of cheap and trashy gossip magazines that we like to flick through and laugh over.

'Wow, I love the coffee table,' I say when I enter the living room. The latest piece of furniture my friend has bought makes her lovely home look even nicer.

'Thanks. It was a bargain, actually. There was a sale at the market last weekend.'

'You got this at the market?'

'Yeah, I know, crazy, right? It's second-hand but it's gorgeous, isn't it? I can't believe what some people throw away.'

I smile at my friend, because this is typical of her. Even though she is doing very well for herself financially, she is not above going down to the local market and picking up an item of previously owned furniture. That's just another thing I love about Leanne. She has no airs or graces and never makes me feel like she is better than me. But if anybody did a comparison study of the pair of us, she would most definitely score higher.

Leanne tells me to make myself comfortable while she goes into the kitchen to get two wine glasses. I do as she says, taking a seat on the sofa, feeling relaxed now that I'm here again. I love this place, and I love hanging out with my best friend. I just wish we could do it as often as we used to. But as we've gotten older, things have changed a little on that front, as they tend to do for so many adults when relationships and work get in the way. While I don't have much going on either front, Leanne certainly is busy. She starts by telling me all about how well things are going in her workplace, which is a fast-paced lawyer's office. Long hours, expensive clients and big bonuses are just a way of life.

'I didn't get home until after midnight on Monday,' my friend tells me with a shake of her head. 'What a start to the week.'

I can scarcely comprehend being needed in a workplace so much that one would be required to work such long hours. I'm certainly not needed that much in mine. But like the considerate friend that she is, Leanne doesn't spend too long talking about herself. She asks me how things are going at my office.

'Yeah, it's fine, I suppose,' I reply, displaying all the weariness of an employee lacking passion for their job.

'Any chance of going full-time like you were hoping for?'

'No, there hasn't been a decision made yet. I guess I have to wait and see, and if not, start looking elsewhere.'

'If you like, I could try again to see if there are any vacancies coming up in our admin team. I know one of the girls there is thinking about leaving, so I might be able to get you in. The pay won't be great to start with, but at least it will be forty hours a week.'

'Thanks, but I'll see how I get on at my place for now.' I brush over that suggestion as politely as I can, because I don't want Leanne to feel like she has to get me a job. I can sort one out for myself. It's very kind of her to want to help, and it's also not the first time she has tried to, but as always, I am pretending that I don't need a helping hand to kick-start my own career.

As fun as it would be to work in the same office as my best friend, I would hate it if Leanne started seeing me as a pathetic loser relying on her to get ahead in life. I also worry that if I worked in her office with all those high-powered lawyers she calls colleagues, then it would only highlight even more how different I am to them. How I possess none of the skills and smarts that they do. Then Leanne might question why she and I are still friends after all these years.

Leanne and I have been best friends since meeting in sixth form college, but while she went on to climb to corporate heights, I stalled and have been stuck in a holding pattern ever since. But there is a good reason for that. I'm not particularly bothered about work and earning loads of money. I know there are more important things in the world than that.

Things like love.

I am in love with Leanne. I've known it since my twenties when I realised that, despite all the guys I was dating, she was the only one I was thinking of. I tried to deny it for as long as

I could, but it was plainly obvious to me that my feelings for her were getting stronger. Even more when I spent time with her.

The problem is that I know Leanne does not feel the same way about me. She has made it clear she is interested in men. Unlike my earliest relationships, which all fizzled out quickly because my heart wasn't in them, Leanne tried to make a good go of things with the men she dated. She even came close to getting married once, back when we were twenty-eight. But then he backtracked on his proposal, saying he needed more time. He delayed the wedding planning as much as possible, and their relationship was never the same again.

Of course, I was relieved that Leanne didn't marry, even though that was selfish of me. But I didn't care at the time. I didn't want to lose her. As long as she stayed single, it would increase the amount of time I got to see her. That is how it transpired as we entered our thirties, and while our respective love lives stalled, Leanne's career did not. But I could cope with that as long as she was happy and still had time for me.

But things changed when she started dating a married man.

It all changed when she met Peter.

And that's whom she is telling me about again now.

'He's taking me away for the night next Wednesday,' Leanne tells me. 'It's just a hotel in town, but we get to spend the whole night together.'

'What has he told his wife?' I ask sceptically.

'He told her that he's going down to London with work.'

I fail to respond to that piece of information. Leanne wisely detects that I'm not comfortable.

'What?' she asks me.

'It's nothing,' I tell her, because I really don't want to have an argument with her.

'No, come on. You can say it. You still think it's a bad idea that I'm seeing him, right?'

'Well, yeah, I do.'

I shrug as I give my honest answer, but it's not really shocking to Leanne. I've expressed my concerns about her and Peter before. I believe that this affair will only end one way: with him choosing his wife over her and Leanne left broken-hearted. And it'll be up to me to pick up the pieces.

'I've told you before, this is serious,' Leanne tells me, putting down her glass of wine hard, as if to emphasise just how much. 'He is going to leave Karen. He's just waiting for the right time.'

'Will there ever be a right time?' I ask. 'I can't imagine he's looking forward to the day he tells his partner and the mother of his children that he is leaving to be with someone else.'

'He is going to do it. He promised me, and I believe him.'

'How do you know he's not lying?'

'He isn't.'

'Isn't he? Look how easily he lies to his wife, telling her that he's going to London on business when he's really going to be shacked up in a hotel around the corner with another woman. He could just as easily be lying to you too.'

'No, he's not like that with me. He loves me.'

I am really trying to keep a lid on my emotions here, but it's extremely difficult, because I feel like my best friend is being the biggest idiot in the world. Maybe if she were just my friend, then I could just keep telling her to be careful. But the fact I have much stronger feelings means I can't control my calm.

'Let's just say he does leave his wife, which I'm still scep-tical about. Look how he cheated on her behind her back.

With you. What would stop him doing the same thing to you when he's bored and has his head turned by another woman?'

'How dare you say that about him! Peter wouldn't do that to me. He loves me!'

It hurts to hear Leanne talk about somebody else loving her who isn't me, especially since I honestly believe Peter has no idea what real love is. If he truly loved Leanne, then he would be here with her now, not me. But my friend is so blind to the truth – in more ways than one. Worse than that, she is now mad at me.

'If you're not going to support me in this, then I'm not sure I can see you,' Leanne tells me.

Her words are like a dagger to my heart. The thought of not being around her is agonising. I have to diffuse this situation quickly before she asks me to leave.

'I'm sorry. I don't mean it to sound like I don't support you. I just don't want you to get hurt, that's all.'

Mercifully, Leanne settles down a little bit, and it doesn't look like I'm going to have to go yet.

'I get that,' she tells me. 'And you know I'm grateful for your concern. But trust me, I'm a big girl, and I know what I'm doing. Peter and I are the real deal. It won't be long until everyone knows it and we don't have to keep things so secretive.'

I still don't really believe that, particularly from Peter's point of view, but I just nod and agree. Because that way I get to stay here in her home rather than going back to my dreary life that feels utterly pointless without Leanne in it.

'What do you think about the idea of me renting this place out as a holiday home?' Leanne suddenly asks me.

'What? Why would you do that?'

'I was just thinking about taking a sabbatical from work and maybe doing a bit of travelling.'

I frown because this is the first I've heard of any desire on Leanne's part to leave the country.

'Really? How long are you thinking?'

'I don't know. Six months, maybe a year.'

'A year?'

'Why not? Work's so busy, and I feel like if I don't do something now, I never will.'

'Where would you go?'

'I don't know. I quite like the sound of South America.'

'South America?' I repeat, processing her words that sound so far away. From me. 'On your own?'

'Not exactly.'

Only then do I realise that this surprising plan might have a little twist that Leanne has not revealed.

'It would be something for Peter and me to do together. He has the option to take a sabbatical too, and I figured it would be a great way to really kick-start the beginning of our relationship – once he's left his wife, of course, and is fully committed to the idea of us.'

I really can't believe this. Not only could I be losing Leanne to a man who doesn't deserve her, but I could be losing her. Out of my life. Completely. If she gets on that plane bound for the other side of the planet, it's a possibility.

'So what do you think?' Leanne asks. 'I could rent this place out, maybe make a little money. Or if not, perhaps you could stay here while I'm away and look after the place. Rent-free, of course.'

I barely hear what Leanne says because I'm still trying to wrap my head around the fact that she could be disappearing out of my life. What the hell am I going to do with myself then?

That evening, it felt like the end of the world.

Little did I know, things were about to get a whole lot worse very soon.

25

PRESENT DAY

I still have a spring in my step after finding out about my competition win, as I wait for Peter to get home from work. I can't believe I was lucky enough to win, but now that I have, I am already plotting what fun my husband and I can get up to with that holiday home to ourselves.

Aware that there is still a lot of work needed to repair our marriage, I think this win could be the perfect opportunity to do some of that in a relaxing environment. And best of all, it won't cost us a penny.

I hear the sound of his key in the front door, and it's perfect timing, because I'm just about to finish making dinner and serve it up. The boys had their meal earlier as usual, and they are playing in their bedrooms before bed. That means there's time for a nice sit-down meal with my partner before then.

'Wow, something smells good,' Peter says as he enters the kitchen and sees my handiwork being dished up.

'You're just in time,' I tell him with a smile before we take a seat at the table and tuck in.

'I have some exciting news,' I say after a couple of mouthfuls of pasta, eager to get it out before he launches into the story about his day.

'Oh, yeah? What's that?' Peter asks.

'I won a competition! A free night's stay at that holiday home I went to last week. How amazing, right?'

'That's great,' Peter says, although he's not quite as enthusiastic about it as I am. Perhaps he's worried I'm going to disappear and leave him with the kids again.

'I know, right? When have I ever won anything?' I ask him, grinning and shaking my head. 'I found out today.'

'So you're going back there again?'

'No, *we're* going back there.'

Peter is surprised by my statement, so I clarify for him.

'I was thinking the two of us could go away for the night. What do you think?'

'What about the kids?'

'I'm sure my parents will agree to do a little babysitting.'

'I suppose.'

'You don't seem keen.'

'No, I am. It sounds great. When are you thinking?'

'Sarah offered a few dates, so we can take a look.'

'That's good,' Peter replies, and he seems to be warming to the idea now. Or maybe he is just feeling better after a hot meal after a long day.

'Yeah, Sarah's really nice. It's very good of her to run a competition like this, don't you think?'

'Yeah, definitely.'

'So I was thinking, when we go to the home, we could take some snacks, some wine, maybe get a takeaway. There's a really cool movie room there in the basement, so we could just gorge ourselves on naughty things and chill out.'

'Sounds perfect.'

'I think so too,' I say with a smile. 'And honestly, the view is to die for. I can't wait for you to see it. Pictures don't even do it justice; that's why I haven't shown you any.'

'Looking forward to it,' Peter says.

I take the hint that he's ready to talk about something else now, because I know when he's losing interest in a conversation topic. I am confident he will be as excited as me when the day arrives to check in to the holiday home and he actually gets to enjoy the surroundings, as well as all the tasty treats we bring with us. But for now, he's more interested in finishing his meal and presumably putting the football match on TV. Kick-off is due shortly.

Once dinner is finished and we tidy away, we make surprisingly quick work of getting the boys into bed. After, Peter sprawls out on the sofa, watching the game, while I message Sarah and ask her when we can claim our free night's stay.

I don't suggest a particular date; I want her to come back and let me know what works for her. I know that my parents will be free to take the kids anytime, so we're pretty flexible. I also know Noah and Oscar will be excited to spend a night at their grandparents', which will make me feel a lot better about being away from them again.

Sarah replies half an hour later, which is good, because I'm falling asleep watching the football match that Peter is engrossed in. When I read her reply, I see that the holiday home is free this Saturday night if we would like it, thanks to a last-minute cancellation.

It is a little short notice, but I think we can do it.

I check with my mum to make sure she is free to have the kids. She is. And I know Peter is free, and he's on for the date when I check with him. So I let Sarah know this weekend works for us, mentioning that my children are excited to stay at their grandparents' and joking that we are equally excited to drop them off there. Sarah responds with a laughing emoji before confirming that we are all booked in, congratulating me one more time and wishing us a lovely stay.

I think Sarah is lovely, and again, I wish there was a way of actually meeting her and thanking her in person. With that in mind, I ask her if she will be around this weekend while we are there, because I would like to say hi and perhaps give her something as a token of our appreciation. I'm sure Peter has a bottle of wine in the cupboard somewhere that we could gift.

But to my disappointment, Sarah responds to say that she has plans this weekend and won't be in the area. She says that her daughter will be getting the home ready for its various guests, so it seems like I won't be putting a face to the name anytime soon.

I message back to tell her it's a shame, but I wish her a good weekend, whatever she is up to. I put my phone down, leaving it at that.

I'm very much looking forward to Saturday night now. Although I make the decision not to mention this to the girls at work. I don't want it to feel like I'm rubbing my win in their faces. I know a couple of them tried to book a stay at the holiday home recently, only to be told that there is limited availability right now. If I tell them, they might be annoyed to find out I am going back again. I guess Sarah prioritises previous guests over new ones, looking after returning customers – or competition winners in my case – like many businesses do. I'm sure my colleagues will get a booking for a stay soon enough. When they do, it will give us something to talk about on our lunch break.

Mercifully, the boring football match comes to a conclusion shortly afterwards. No need for the thirty minutes of extra time. Peter and I watch something a little more interesting before we retire to bed just after eleven. The kids have been well behaved tonight, and there have been no dramas with sneaking out of bed or getting themselves locked in the bathroom again. For that, I am grateful.

I am also grateful that my confidence has returned enough to invite Peter to sleep in our bed again. It feels like we turned the corner now, and with Saturday night to look forward to, I am feeling optimistic.

I turn out the bedroom light and snuggle under my duvet, with him beside me.

Bring on the weekend.

It promises to be a fun one.

26

EVE

I t's funny how when people are so desperate to be called a winner, they will believe anything.

Since telling Karen that she won my competition and can come and stay this weekend at relatively short notice, the ecstatic woman hasn't stopped telling me about it, wondering if all this might be too good to be true. Not even the knowledge of her work colleagues struggling to book a date can dampen her excitement. She's been blinded by the fact that, for the first time in her miserable life, she won something. But she's not the only winner today. I'm a winner too.

As I prepare the house for the arrival of Karen and her husband, I am closer to seeing some tangible reward for all of my efforts.

To get everything ready, I started with the boring stuff, like cleaning the house and putting out the champagne and chocolates again. It's tedious, but it's all necessary to keep up the pretence. I also found myself whistling while I vacuumed and dusted. I took it as a sign that, despite everything I went through, my plan for revenge is improving my state of mind.

I have no doubts that I would not be alive today if I hadn't decided to punish Peter. Suicide is a strong word, and it makes me uncomfortable to think that I might have gone through with it. If I hadn't started all of this, then I firmly believe I would have. Things had become unbearable, and suicide felt like my only way out. But now I have found another way.

That I am here whistling proves everything is okay again.

It's funny how quickly things can change.

With Karen and Peter's check-in only an hour away, the pair will be forced to think a lot about how quickly things change once their stay is over. To make that happen, I really need to start wrapping things up here. I can't be here when they arrive.

Leaving the pristine interior of the house behind, I walk across the driveway to the garage and lift up the heavy, white door. Inside the space, I see some of the usual things that one would expect to find in a garage, like a lawnmower, a set of hedge clippers and a piece of furniture that really should be taken to the local dump. But I also see the one thing I have been storing in here, ready for tonight, and I pick it up before leaving the garage.

I don't like to spend a second longer than I need to in that garage because of the part it played in Leanne's death. Leanne's father got quite the shock when he discovered his daughter in there after wondering why he hadn't heard from her in a while.

It sends chills through me to think of my best friend hanging in that dank, damp room, which is why I don't like going in there.

Placing the item in my backpack, I set it on the ground outside the front door. Then I make one final check on the property before feeling confident that it is ready. I leave the key in the lockbox, where Karen and Peter can access it, before picking up my bulky backpack, which now contains a red jerrycan, and calling a taxi. I also managed to stuff a few items of clothing in before that so I have something to change into later.

The balaclava will be the item of clothing I'll need most.

The taxi arrives, and I get in the back. The driver drops me off at the petrol station around the corner from the hostel and drives off. I need to fill up my jerrycan with fuel. I stick one of the pump nozzles into the can and press carefully until I have enough fuel for what I need to do.

I go inside the station to pay for the petrol, and once that is done, I head down the quiet street that I already spent time scoping out earlier in the week. I was looking for somewhere close by that had plenty of bushes in which to hide this jerrycan, and was quiet enough so there was less chance of somebody coming along and finding it.

After hiding the jerrycan amongst the bushes and covering it up with leaves and branches, I am confident that it will still be there when I return tonight under the cover of darkness. Then I set off for the hostel, but before I return to that bedbug-ridden place, I make one final stop. I call in at a small convenience store and buy a packet of matches. I buy these because having fuel isn't going to be much good to me if I have nothing to ignite it with.

I feel satisfied that by buying the items separately, nobody will connect me to the blaze that is likely to make the head-lines in this town. Now all I have to do is lie on my hostel bed and wait for the sun to set. But I won't be bored while I do that because the cameras in the house are still active. I'll be able to watch as Karen and Peter check in and make them-selves comfortable. Having already watched Karen before, I feel confident I can predict what she will get up to there. But it is Peter whom I am more intrigued by, because I haven't seen him in my environment yet. I am very much looking forward to gauging his reaction to the property when he enters it.

I expect he will be shocked when he sees where his wife has him staying for the night.

It won't feel like a holiday for him, that's for sure.

I check in with the sleepy young man at the check-in desk in the hostel, who seems surprised that I am a returning customer. I presume it's because they never get such a thing.

I head up to my allocated room in a mixed dorm – the only type this hostel has. It's a different room to the last one I stayed in, but the bunk beds are just as creaky and uncomfortable, and there are just as many strangers as last time.

A bearded, middle-aged man watches me as I enter and claim my allocated bed. He asks me if I have a husband and, if not, would I like to go for a drink with him. I politely decline his invitation before he goes back to looking at the magazine in his hands, which is for motorsports enthusiasts, so holds little interest for me.

But my phone is my entertainment for this afternoon.

I make sure to have the app open on my device, and watch through the camera that covers the driveway of Leanne's home. I'm waiting for Karen and Peter to park outside the house and to get out with their luggage. I wonder if Karen has packed more than last time or less. It should be less, considering that she is only staying for one night, but it could be more because she might have packed a little lingerie for this evening.

If so, I'm sure Peter is expecting a fun night ahead.

How wrong he will be about that.

27

PETER

The steep drive to the holiday home following Karen's directions is giving me two things. It's giving me a taste of the spectacular views my wife mentioned. It's also giving me heart palpitations.

I recognise this area.

I have been up here before. I never ever thought I would be back.

But every direction that Karen gives is taking me closer and closer to a place that I really don't want to be. But there are several houses around here, and I pray that we will be going to a different one.

That is until Karen tells me to take a left turn, and then we arrive.

My worst fears are confirmed.

I'm back at this house again.

The house that belonged to the woman I had an affair with.

Through the windscreen I stare at the property as Karen asks me what my first impressions of the place are. But what can I say to that? I certainly can't say that I've been here before and know what every room in this house looks like.

Not only that, but I've slept in one of the beds here and taken a shower here, and neither of those activities were done alone.

And while my wife knows about my affair, she doesn't know where Leanne lived. I just told her it was a house across town and left it at that. But now we are right outside that house, and bizarrely, the home my mistress once lived is the same place my wife chose to go on holiday, not once but twice.

This can't be right. Something is wrong here.

Is Karen playing games with me? Did she bring me back here to make me uncomfortable?

Did she somehow find out where Leanne lived and is now using that information to make me feel even guiltier about what I did?

I don't know. I guess it is possible.

But why would she do that? Playing games is not something my wife does, so why start now? When she discovered the affair, she didn't mess me around, even though she had every right to. She kept everything simple and straightforward. She wanted to know when the affair started, why it happened and, most importantly, if it was over. Since then, she has made little mention of it. It took most of this last year to smooth things between us, but I feel like we are getting there. So it doesn't make sense for Karen to suddenly drag us all the way back to that dark period in our relationship.

She said we would move forward.

Yet here I am going backwards again.

'Well?' Karen says after I fail to answer her question. 'What do you think?'

'Erm, yeah. It's nice,' I mutter as I look at the house and get flashbacks of the times I came here before.

Like the night I came here in a taxi with Leanne, and we barely made it through the front door before we ripped each other's clothes off. Or the time I called around here on my lunch hour, walked in, and we took a bath together. This place holds so many memories for me, and while they were good ones at the time, they are bad ones now that carry so much guilt and remorse. I deeply regret what I did to Karen, and really want to put the affair behind me.

But how can I do that when I'm in the one place that won't let me forget about the past?

I turn and look at my wife sitting beside me. I try to get a read on her to figure out whether she knows my history with this place. She smiles at me, genuinely and warmly, before opening the car door and getting out.

If she does, then she is doing a good job of concealing it.

I'm still none the wiser as to whether my wife is messing with me, so all I can do is the same as her. I get out and grab our luggage from the boot; then she shows me where the lockbox is with the key inside.

Karen explains how the current owner uses the lockbox, and while it all sounds stress-free and convenient, all I can think about is the previous owner of this property.

I know that Leanne is dead now, and I also know why she is gone – not that I spend much time dwelling on that grim reason. I guess the house was sold, and this woman called Sarah is the new owner. Perhaps she is one of those wealthy people who buys up new properties and then rents them out in one form or another, cleverly making other people pay off her mortgage. That would be the most logical explanation for all of this. It could just be sheer bad luck that my wife ended up finding out about this place and booking a stay here.

But do I believe in bad luck? Yeah. It was bad luck that Karen found that receipt in my trouser pocket and unravelled my affair. But that slice of luck pales in comparison to what is happening now.

'Here we go,' Karen says as she collects the key from the lockbox and heads over to the front door.

I follow behind her, but my legs feel like they're made of lead, and each step is torturous to me. I don't want to go inside, even if Karen is genuinely naïve as to what this place represents in our marriage's sordid history. But I'm hardly going to enlighten my wife, am I?

If she is oblivious, it's because I never told her where Leanne lived. Nor did I ever mention Leanne's name. Therefore, I can't tell Karen that my mistress used to live here. I guess I'm just going to have to live with the discomfort until we leave here.

I hate lying to my wife, and I promised myself I never would again, but I'm forced to once again while Karen shows me around the home. I have to pretend to be impressed with the interior, which I've seen before, just like I have to fake how stunned I am by the lovely view she shows me on the terrace, which Leanne and I used to admire together.

'Wow, it's amazing,' I say, doing my best to sound impressed, while at the same time doing my best not to think about the time Leanne and I had sex on this terrace, just over a year ago.

The longer we spend in this house, the more assured I am that Karen really has no clue Leanne lived here. She is too relaxed for that and seems genuinely happy to be here with me. Now she is opening the champagne and prompting me to take a chocolate, as if this really is just a fun night away for us, so I grab a chocolate and make sure not to ruin it for her.

When she hands me a glass of bubbles, she toasts to us before suggesting we check out the movie room in the basement.

As I follow my wife downstairs, my heart races. I push away all thoughts about the time Leanne led me down to this same room before she locked us in, telling me that she wouldn't let me leave until I promised her I would leave Karen soon. I thought at the time that Leanne was joking and laughed. And when Leanne smiled and unlocked that door, I believed her. But as time went on, it became clear that she was getting serious about me leaving Karen. Her troubling change of mood, combined with Karen's discovery of my affair, hastened my decision to stop it.

I've not been back to this house since.

And I know that is why Leanne is not here.

Karen puts on a movie, and I do my best to appear relaxed on the sofa next to her. I sip my champagne; the alcohol, plus the film, makes it a little easier to forget about my anxieties. It's not like Leanne can walk in on us.

But I am still dreading the thought of going upstairs and sleeping in Leanne's room with my wife. Too many memories in that bed.

Perhaps it is just a cruel twist of fate and destiny that brings me back here one more time. My punishment for my past mistakes. I can't say I don't deserve it. But I can say that I cannot wait for this trip to be over.

We're halfway through the movie when Karen starts kissing me. While it is enjoyable, it's almost impossible to see anyone but Leanne. We did this in this exact same spot. Karen pulls back a moment later, and the look on her face suggests she senses something might be wrong. I quickly assure her that I'm fine, and we kiss some more.

As hard as it is to do this here, I know that I mustn't mess this up. Karen is returning to how she was with me before my affair, and I need to latch onto the progress made and preserve it. When Karen tells me to put down my champagne and says we should go upstairs, I know what is on her mind.

I nod and allow her to lead me to the master bedroom. It looks so neat and presentable – as any bedroom in a holiday home would be. The made bed doesn't stay picture-perfect for long because Karen pulls the duvet back and invites me to get in.

We kiss under the covers and remove each other's clothes, and I try to focus on the woman I am with now and not the woman I used to be in this bed with. She's in the past; Karen is my present and my future.

I count down the hours to when we will be packed and driving away from here.

I just want to get back to my own house because there's no place like home.

But I'm not the only one who knows that.

28

EVE

My anger flares as I watch Karen and Peter defile the bed where my best friend used to sleep. They move beneath the sheets, directly below the hidden camera I put in the light fitting above the bed. My trembling hand squeezes my mobile phone.

I could throw the device away, such is my level of annoyance, but I know that won't do any good.

I also know there is something much better I can do to improve my mood.

Scrolling through my phone, I find the app that allows me to control the alarm system installed in the house. I set the timer, to give the occupants ten seconds to leave before the motion sensors are activated. I haven't been setting the alarm while Karen has been staying at the house – it would be too much hassle to explain to her how it worked – but the time has come to give her and Peter a little lesson now.

I count down while watching the feed, waiting for the ten seconds to elapse and for the writhing couple to trigger the sensors and be deafened by the loud, blaring alarm. The countdown is silent in the house, so Karen and Peter have no idea what is about to happen. They continue to writhe. But they will know about it very shortly.

I see Peter rise suddenly in the bed and look around. A second later, an alarm trigger notification comes through on my phone. Knowing everything is fine at the house, I smile and watch the pair of them trying to figure out what to do.

Peter is out of bed now and heading for the door, in nothing but his boxer shorts, while Karen remains in bed, entangled in the sheets and covering her ears. I can't hear the noise at my end, but I heard it before once, when I accidentally triggered the alarm, and it is certainly deafening.

I doubt there are many things more conducive to killing the mood in the bedroom than a high-pitched noise. I check the other cameras in the house and see Peter scampering around in his boxers, trying to find the cause. He must have figured out it's the house alarm. He rushes to the door in the hallway, because he knows precisely where that alarm is located. I'm guessing he saw Leanne turn it off or on during one of his previous visits here. The fact that he is still in the house now rather than returned home suggests he didn't tell his wife about where Leanne lived.

What a shock.

Peter fumbles in the hallway cupboard, trying to find a way to shut the alarm off, but he won't have any success.

There are only two ways to stop the noise. Either he enters the code on the alarm's keypad – which he won't know because I changed it recently – or I press a button on my phone that will cancel it.

But I'm not going to press that button yet.

Not until I've messed with them a little more.

I put my phone away and leave the hostel with my backpack. I don't plan on taking it out again until I get a phone call from Karen, which I expect will happen in a few minutes' time, asking Sarah how to turn the alarm off. My backpack holds only two items after I unpacked the clothes and left them on my bed in the hostel – the box of matches I bought earlier, and the balaclava I will be using shortly to conceal my face.

It doesn't take me long to reach the spot where I hid the jerrycan, and I'm relieved to see it undisturbed when I pull back the foliage and carefully put it into my backpack. Then I set off for the house, already aware that it will take me precisely eleven minutes, because I did a test run three times already.

I'm four minutes closer to my destination when I hear my phone ringing. I check the caller ID, and I see my earlier prediction is right on time.

Karen is trying to get hold of me.

The helpful thing now would be to answer her call and play along, using a fake voice and pretending I am Sarah, and help her turn off the alarm that is ruining her romantic evening with her husband. And that's precisely why I don't answer the call.

I'm choosing to be frustrating rather than friendly.

It's a couple of minutes later when I get a text message from Karen, telling me something I already know.

Hi. Really sorry to bother you, but the house alarm is going off, and we don't know why, or how to stop it. Please can you give me a call? It's very loud!

I smirk at Karen's description of the volume, then make a check on the pair to see what they're doing right now, and whether they are wearing a little more clothing now. When I find them, I see they are both standing in the hallway; Karen is in her husband's baggy T-shirt while he is still just in his boxer shorts. They haven't progressed much on the alarm front, and despite the pair still looking at the panel in the cupboard, I know it's still going off. Why? Because my phone is telling me. So is the visual of Karen sticking her fingers in her ears.

I decide that I have toyed with them enough, and I know I can't push it much further, or else they might leave, so I press the button that resets the alarm. Then I type out a quick reply to Karen, in which I apologise for the disturbance and that it must be a glitch with the security panel. She takes a moment to reply, probably because she is still regaining her hearing, before letting me know that the alarm has stopped, and everything is okay now.

I laugh at her choice of words, because little does she know that everything is *not* okay. At least not in her world anyway. That's because I am almost at my destination, and when I get there, I will be removing the three items from my backpack and putting them all to good use.

The balaclava will cover my head; the fuel in the jerrycan will go through the letterbox; a single match will be lit and will follow the fuel. Then I will make myself scarce, making sure to be away from the house before it is completely engulfed in flames. But I won't go far. I will watch from a safe place as the house burns, because I deserve to watch my plan reach its conclusion.

The sight of Karen and Peter's home burning will bring a smile to my balaclava-clad face, and not just because it will be fun to see that place wiped off the map. It will be fun because at the exact time it is burning, neither Karen nor Peter will have any idea what is happening. They will most likely be too busy sipping champagne, watching a movie, or perhaps returning to the bedroom to finish what they started earlier.

But make no mistake; there will come a time soon when the reality of what is about to happen here will dawn on them. And then the fun will be over, at least for them anyway.

But I'll still be smiling.

And I don't expect to stop anytime soon.

29

KAREN

My ears are still ringing from the high-pitched sound, but now the alarm is off, Peter and I can try to go back to our relaxing break. It's a shame our lovemaking was interrupted by the alarm, but hopefully later we can pick up where we left off. For now, I'm content with taking a seat on the sofa and plotting out the next part of our mini-holiday.

'What do you fancy for dinner?' I ask Peter as I recline on the sofa. 'There are a few takeaways nearby.'

'I'm easy,' he says as he moves through the room, but he doesn't seem anywhere near as relaxed as I am.

'What's wrong?'

'Nothing.'

'You look tense.'

'I'm fine.'

'Come and have a seat.'

'In a minute.'

With that Peter goes into the kitchen, and I'm left alone in the living room to wait for his return. I guess he's still a little agitated from the alarm. It was certainly a shock to hear it come on. But I worry it could be something else bothering him, so I go into the kitchen and check up on him. I see him sitting at the table, flicking through the review book.

'What are you doing?' I ask him, even though it's obvious.

'Just seeing what other people have said about this place,' he replies. He flicks through the pages at the front, as if he's looking for the earliest review.

'They're all positive,' I tell him and slide onto the chair beside him. 'Well, apart from the odd one or two.'

'What did they say?'

'Nothing much. You know some people; they have to find something to complain about.'

Peter doesn't smile and continues flicking through the book. After a quiet moment of me watching him reading reviews, I'm still worried that something is bothering him.

'What's the matter? Do you not like it here?'

'No, of course I do,' he replies a little defensively.

'You seem a little off.'

'I'm fine, I promise.'

'Are you sure something isn't bothering you? Was it the alarm? Or was it what we were doing before it went off?'

My last question is a slightly needy one, but I ask it anyway. It's better to be vulnerable and aware than to bury one's head in the sand and pretend like everything is okay. If it isn't okay, then I would rather know than carry on in blissful ignorance.

Was my husband not enjoying himself when we were in bed together?

Peter looks up suddenly from the review book and right at me, as if he is snapping back to the moment.

'Don't be silly. Everything was fine.'

'Fine?'

'I mean it was great!'

He takes my hand, as if to prove that everything is perfect between us.

'So what is it, then?' I ask. 'Because something is troubling you, so don't try to deny it.'

I stare at my husband, waiting for his response, feeling some of that old fear I had back when I first found that hotel receipt in his trouser pocket. It's the same fear that he might be keeping another secret. And even though I could let it go and not demand to know what it is, I can't. I have to ask, for my peace of mind.

'You were right the first time,' he confesses a moment later, taking his hand from mine. 'It's this place.'

That the problem is this house rather than anything between us is a relief.

'You don't like it?'

'It's not that I don't like it.'

'What, then?'

Peter lets out a deep sigh before answering me.

'It's just not home, is it?'

It takes me a few seconds to get what he means, but when I do, a big smile spreads across my face.

'You're missing the kids?' I ask him. He shrugs before giving me a sheepish nod.

I laugh then, and it's a way of letting out some of the nervous tension I've had since following him in here. It's not bad news. He doesn't have another deep, dark secret to share with me. In fact, it's good news. He is just being a loving dad and wants to see his boys again, even though we only left them at my parents' house a couple of hours ago.

'That's so sweet,' I tell him and take his hand. 'I miss them too. But I think it's important we have this time to ourselves.'

'We could just go home and do that,' Peter suggests. 'The kids are out. We don't necessarily need to stay here to be alone together.'

'Well, yeah, I guess. But isn't it nice to have a change of scenery?'

'Yeah, it is. But it might be more relaxing in our own home. There are no alarms going off there.'

'I'm sure it won't go off again.'

'Maybe. Maybe not.'

I pull my hand back, because now I am convinced his problem with being here doesn't just stem from him missing our sons.

'What's going on?' I ask him.

'Huh? Nothing.'

I wish I could take that answer at face value, but the grunt he made just before saying 'nothing' was a tell that he *is* hiding something. That's because it's the exact same noise he made when I first produced the hotel receipt and asked him about it. It's the sound he makes when he is trying to act like everything is okay when it isn't.

'I thought we said we weren't going to keep any more secrets,' I say with a shake of the head.

'We aren't.'

'I know *I'm* not,' I say, getting up from the table to make a point.

'Karen. Wait.'

But I ignore my husband and walk out of the room, even though I know there isn't anywhere for me to really escape to, considering we're holed away in this holiday home together. Sure enough, Peter follows me and catches up before I can make it up the stairs.

'There's nothing wrong. Seriously,' he tries again.

'Stop lying to me.'

'I'm not!'

'Something's bothering you. I can tell.'

'I told you. I'm missing the boys.'

'You told me how much you were looking forward to a

break when we were driving here.'

'I know, but I didn't think I'd miss them this much. It's the same as when you came home early from here because you missed them, remember?'

'No, that's not it. You were fine on the way here, but you've been off ever since we checked in.'

'What do you mean?'

'I don't know. I can just tell something's bothering you.'

Peter says, 'Everything was fine until that damn alarm went off.'

'No, that's not it. You were distracted before that. I didn't say anything because I didn't want to cause an argument, but I could tell.'

'So you're causing an argument now?'

'I just want you to be honest with me.'

'I am!'

'So what's wrong with this house?'

'Nothing!'

'Fine!'

I stomp up the stairs, needing to get away from Peter before we get into a real argument. I can't believe we're fighting on our one night away. While I am aware that I'm the one who started it, I did because I can tell Peter is hiding something from me. The fact he won't just tell me convinces me the house isn't really the problem here, but me.

Does he regret coming away with me? Did he not enjoy himself in the bedroom before? Can he not love me as hard as I'm trying to love him, after everything that happened?

I reach the bedroom and see the tangled bedsheets – a reminder of what we were doing before that damn alarm went off. If only it hadn't sounded, then maybe things could still be okay. But now we're arguing, and I'm not sure what we do next.

Do we stay here or go home?

30

EVE

Karen and Peter's street is quiet as I make my way down it, in the direction of their house. I walked here after deciding it was too risky to call a cab and have the driver recall at a later date seeing me here. This part of town puts me very much in middle-class suburbia, but predictably, at this time of night, everybody is safely tucked away in their homes, with their nice cars parked in the driveways and their expensive TVs glowing through the windows.

I wonder what it must be like to have enough money to own a nice house like this, or to have a good car and the peace of mind to put one's feet up at the end of the day and lose oneself in a good TV show or film. That's certainly not my reality.

What I own in this world is either in the backpack I'm carrying or lying on that lumpy hostel bed. It's been a long time since I felt relaxed enough to be entertained by a little fiction. Unlike all the people here, I am like a mangy, hungry coyote, stalking the streets after dark. But it's not food I am seeking. It is revenge. And now that I'm outside Karen and Peter's house, I am about to get it.

I visually check that all the lights are off inside the home before I creep up the dark driveway and to the side of the house. Now that I am definitely out of view of anybody on this street who might peep through their curtains, I take out the heavy can of fuel and the matches, then pull the balaclava over my head.

The material feels uncomfortable against my skin, but I know I won't have to wear my disguise for long. I creep to the front of the house and make another check on the street.

All is quiet.

But that's about to change.

Unscrewing the lid from the jerrycan, I walk towards the front door, taking care not to spill any of the strong-smelling fuel. Then I push open the letterbox, hearing it creak slightly. But it's not loud enough to draw the attention of the neighbours. They wouldn't hear the sound over the noise of their TVs. But I imagine they *will* hear the sirens when the fire brigade arrives soon.

Tipping the contents carefully, I pour the fuel through the letterbox and hear it splash onto the floor. I keep pouring until the jerrycan is empty. I put the can down and light a match. It's a nervous moment for me, because it's hard not to imagine myself going up in a ball of flames. But I took my time so I wouldn't get petrol on me; that isn't going to happen.

I won't be burning.

But this house is about to go up in flames.

After dropping the lit match through the letterbox, I step back. I hear a loud whoosh as the petrol ignites; then I see the orange glow growing through the stained-glass window to the side of the front door. I'm happy the fire has started, and I'm confident it will do considerable damage before the firefighters get here and are able to put out the flames.

Returning the empty can and the matches to my rucksack, I scurry down the driveway, resisting the temptation to look back until I am at a much safer distance. When I feel confident that I am far enough away from the house, I stop on the street corner, take off the balaclava and look back.

I can see the orange glow from here, and the fire is really taking hold now. But there will be no 999 call until somebody else on this street sees it. By then, I imagine it will be too late to save the house.

As I watch the fire grow, I think about Karen and Peter still at the holiday home, blissfully unaware that everything they ever worked for is going up in flames. What a shock it will be for them when they receive a phone call to let them know that something terrible happened. They will have to find somewhere else to live. I imagine that somewhere else will be Karen's parents' place, which is where Noah and Oscar are spending the night this evening. The disruption this fire is going to cause to my targets' lives, as well as the suffering they will feel at losing the place that they call home, is a source of great comfort to me, but it doesn't mean I am done with them yet.

Not by a long way.

Checking the camera footage on my phone, I look to see what Karen and Peter are doing right now. But when I do, I get a little surprise. They are both in the house, but they are in separate rooms. Karen is lying on Leanne's bed, reading a book, while Peter is in the basement, watching a movie.

That's strange. I would have thought they'd be spending every second of their break together, making the most of being away from the kids. It certainly seemed like they were trying to take advantage of the situation before I set that alarm off.

But something obviously happened between them. I wonder if they had a fight. It's possible, but what about? Did

Peter tell Karen about his history with the house? No, Karen would have left if he did. It must be something else, then. Whatever it is, it seems things are a little frosty between them. In that moment Peter crosses his arms, with a grumpy expression on his face.

But there's nothing chilly about the atmosphere in the house down the street from me. I look back up and see the fiery glow has spread from the hallway into the living room. That's the room where Peter and I shared a glass of wine not so long ago, but it will be a long time before anybody sits in there and has a drink again.

Another five minutes pass before I see a next-door neighbour pulling their curtains open. An old lady peers out of her window. I imagine she noticed the bright light emanating from nearby and is checking on it. She must have got a shock.

The old woman disappears from view, and I presume she is rushing to her telephone now to call the emergency services. I wonder what their response time will be, but every second they aren't here is another second for Karen and Peter's house to become even more unrecognisable.

I'm starting to smell smoke now from my position behind the hedge several hundred yards away. But I'm no longer the only one being morbidly entertained, because several doors open on the street, and neighbours step outside to watch the drama unfolding on their doorstep.

There are several shakes of the head as well as a few moans of anguish from the various residents. The reality of the situation is dawning on them. I'm sure this will give them something to gossip about in the coming days. I imagine there isn't much that elicits interest and intrigue in this part of town, but this street will certainly be getting a mention in the local newspaper tomorrow. I can already see some junior journalist knocking on doors, looking for a few eyewitness accounts.

The sound of sirens peals in the distance while the crackle from the fire gets louder. By the time I see the fire engines speeding down the street, the property is ablaze and almost certainly unrecoverable.

The firefighters emerge from their vehicles and work in unison to pull out the water hoses. They are efficient and well-trained, but they're not miracle workers, and despite their valiant efforts, it still takes a surprising amount of time to put the flames out. I spent that time like a few other people did on this street, taking a few sneaky photos to look back on at a later date. But eventually, the fun is over and the fire is out, leaving the once pretty house nothing more than a burnt and blackened shell that no sane person would ever want to set foot in.

I guess there's only one thing left for the brave firefighters to do.

They have to let the homeowners know what happened to their home.

31

The champagne in my glass has gone flat, much like the atmosphere in this house. While I'm not sure what I can do about the latter problem, I can do something about the former.

I walk into the kitchen and pour what is left of my drink down the sink. The silence in this house lets me know that Karen is most likely still upstairs sulking after our earlier disagreement. That's a problem and one I'm not sure how best to solve.

I guess I should go up there and see how she is doing. We can't stay like this all night, stewing in separate rooms until the sun comes up and it's time for us to collect our belongings and head home. Doing that will render this entire trip a waste of time. But before I leave the kitchen and go in search of my disgruntled wife, I spot the review book on the table again. I decide to take another look inside it.

I already read some of the things inside it, but I was interrupted by Karen, so I open the book now to the first page and look for any hint of a date. I'm trying to see when these reviews began, because that will give me some indication as to how long it was after Leanne's death before this place started being used as a holiday home.

But the first review doesn't have a date on it, nor does the second. However, I get a bit of luck with the third one; one guest wrote that they enjoyed a lovely summer day in this place. I can only assume they are referring to a date around the middle part of last year. That would suggest this place was opened up to guests three or four months or so after Leanne passed.

It seems a little too quick. Did Leanne's family really put their grief aside that quickly to cash in on this place? Did they sell it, or perhaps hire Sarah to run it as a holiday home?

Possibly. I didn't trawl through the estate agency listings after Leanne's death to see if this place went up for sale, changed hands or was listed on some holiday home website. I just wanted to forget about it, to be honest. But it's proving impossible to do that now that I am here.

I read a few more reviews, but there aren't any more that pinpoint specific times or dates that could help me build a better picture of how this house has been used since I was last here. I guess it all seems legit so far, but it's still spooking me out. It's spooking me out the same amount as the day I got the news that my ex-mistress killed herself.

I'll never forget where I was and what I was doing when I found out Leanne took her own life. I was at a garden centre with Noah and Oscar, and we were shopping for plants for the garden. Karen was at home, getting the house tidy after another typical chaotic few days in our house. My eager sons picked out several things they wanted to have a go at planting, and the items were in the trolley that I was pushing when I my phone rang.

I presumed it was my wife calling me to check up on us, because we were at that garden centre a while. It's not easy to locate two young boys who like to run around a large outdoor place with lots of aisles and lots of hiding places. But it wasn't Karen calling me. It was from a number I didn't recognise. But when I answered it, I found out exactly who it was.

It was the police.

And they wanted me to come to the station.

I guess some people might be so afraid to receive such a call that they would immediately follow the officer's orders. But I didn't do that. Instead, I demanded to know what the call was about, telling the officer over the phone that I had my two young boys with me, and I couldn't just abandon my duties unless I knew why it had to be done.

It took a few minutes before the officer explained why I had to come and speak to them. It was because the body of Leanne Reeves had been discovered, and while her death was not being treated a suspicious, they wished to interview me because of what had been found beside her body.

It was a letter.

With my name on it.

I finished up quickly at the garden centre after that and took the boys home. I told Karen I had to go to the office because a colleague called and asked me to pick something up for them. It was another lie, and a lousy one at that, but there would be time for telling the truth later. In that moment, I just needed to get to the station and find out what Leanne had done.

Hearing she died was a shock, and not just because she was younger than me. It was because she had been making threats for a while, threatening to do something stupid, since I told her I was not leaving my wife for her and that I wanted the affair to end. But I never thought Leanne would seriously go through with her threats. I just figured she was heart-broken and needed some time, like many people do when a relationship ends. But when I arrived at the station and went into a private room with the officer who called me, I learnt that Leanne had been deadly serious.

She'd committed suicide, and the letter next to her body explained exactly why she came to her grim decision. She named me in it, and it said that if I didn't want her, then she didn't want to live. She went on to say how she wished she had never met me and that her life had been ruined by being 'the other woman'.

I felt extreme shame as I sat there, opposite that police officer, listening to them detail private parts of my affair, details that Leanne openly shared in the letter. My phone number was also in it because she made it clear in the letter that she wanted me to know exactly what I drove her to do. I felt shame because I was responsible for someone else's death, and while the police weren't going to charge me with anything, that didn't make it any easier to process. I left the station and returned home to my family.

It was later that night when the children were in bed that Karen demanded to know the truth for my disappearance. She hadn't really bought the 'going into the office' explanation. I told her what had happened to Leanne. Karen was shocked, just like I was, and I feared it could be the tipping point that heralded the end of our relationship. Could she live with the knowledge of what her unfaithful husband's actions led someone else to do? Could I live with that knowledge too?

All this time later and we are still together, so I guess we somehow managed it. But things are still far from right, and for Leanne and her family, they never will be.

I decide to talk to my wife and see if I can make things better with her. We've been through too much that I'm not going to let us spend tonight apart when we should be together. But as I make my way up the stairs, I hear my phone ringing. When I check the caller ID, I see another number I don't recognise.

The sight of it is enough to give me horrible flashbacks to that day in the garden centre, but surely it's a coincidence. I can't be getting bad news twice in this manner.

But then I answer the call and listen to a neighbour tell me what happened.

There's been a fire, and we need to go home.

Or at least we need to return to what is left of our home.

32

I t's still dark when the police car parks up outside what's left of our house; it looks very different to all the other houses on this street. As I stare through the window at the blackened and burnt-out building, I feel my chest tighten so much, I have to grip the door handle for support. Peter was right when he told me that something terrible had happened. The police officer who picked us up from the holiday home and offered his apologies for what happened was also right.

This really is a nightmare.

And it is unfolding right before my eyes.

I look around at all the emergency service vehicles parked on this street – further evidence that this quiet part of town was a hive of activity while Peter and I were elsewhere. There are investigators from the crime scene, police and even a couple of paramedics standing by a parked ambulance watching on – the latter not needed, thankfully, but hanging around just in case. The kids weren't here at the time, so that is one small mercy in what is otherwise a devastating event.

Possessions and property can be replaced, but people

can't. That's what the police officer said as he drove us home. Of course he was right, and I am extremely grateful that this fire did not occur when we were all at home. But it's still a sobering sight to see our beautiful home destroyed.

I can feel my legs shaking as I make my way to the edge of the driveway with Peter beside me, but we are stopped from going any farther by the firefighters. Even though the fire has been put out, there is still too much smoke, and it is far too unsafe for us to go inside. But as sensible as that sounds, it's not good enough for me.

I want to see the damage for myself.

I want to check on all the rooms that I know so well.

I want to see it all, however devastating it might be.

But Peter is a little more level-headed than me, and he stops me from arguing with the firefighters, who are just doing their job. The police officer grabs our attention, saying he has something he wants to tell us.

'We're still trying to determine the cause of the fire, but it appears it began in the hallway,' he says.

'Did it spread through the entire house?' I ask.

The officer grimly nods his head. 'I'm afraid so. It seems it was a particularly aggressive fire. But we are investigating the cause and will give you more information when we have it.'

'What the hell could have started it?' Peter wants to know but gets no answer.

'It was a good thing that you were out,' we are then told. 'But because the property was empty, it gave the fire an opportunity to spread faster before the alarm was raised. By the time we arrived here, it had already consumed most of the building.'

'I can't believe this,' Peter mumbles, shaking his head.

'I understand this is a very difficult time for you.'

I have to hold my tongue because I feel like telling this officer off, that he cannot possibly understand how difficult it is for us. But maybe he can, because he presumably attends all sorts of fires all over town and had to have this same conversation with numerous other people during his career. But while that might make it easier for him to see stuff like this, this is my first time dealing with a house fire. That's why my body continues to shake and my heart continues to hammer in my chest.

'Is there somewhere you can stay?' he asks us then, and I mumble something back about my parents' house.

He leaves, and I'm barely paying attention, because I still can't believe this happened. I know my parents will let us stay with them until we can sort something out, but we shouldn't have to stay anywhere else. We should be staying here. This is our home. This is where my family and I belong.

'How are we going to tell the boys?' I ask Peter. We are both staring at the remains of the life we built.

'I'll tell them,' he replies quietly.

'All our clothes. Our photos. Our memories. Gone.'

'We're all safe. That's the main thing.'

'But how do we come back from this? How do we start again?'

'I don't know.'

My eyes are stinging as they fill with fresh tears, but it could also be because the air is thick with smoke. The longer I stand here, the more I begin to choke on the acrid air. It doesn't help that I can see several of our neighbours watching from outside their homes, or peeping through their curtains. I get that this is a big deal, but could they not gawk like that?

How about they have a little respect for what we lost here.

I want to shout out and tell them to mind their own business, but I manage to restrain myself, aware that getting emotional will only create even more of a scene. There's enough going on already without me adding to the drama.

'I need to get out of here,' I say to Peter and turn away

from the upsetting sight of my gutted house. I look for the police car that brought us here. 'We need to go to my parents'. Now.'

Peter agrees with me and tells me he wants to speak to one of the police officers first, to find out what happens next. So I wait for him to return, feeling numb, confused and shocked by what happened tonight.

The evening was already on a downward trajectory ever since our argument at the holiday home, but I could scarcely have imagined how things would go from bad to worse a few hours later. But it's not just tonight that has me feeling beaten. After the year I had since finding out about Peter's affair, this is just another heart-wrenching ordeal to try to overcome.

Why do bad things keep happening to me? What did I do to deserve any of this? But just like when I asked myself the same thing after learning of my husband's infidelity, I still have no idea why. I'm not a bad person. I haven't done anything that could attract this kind of karma. I'm just a mother and wife trying to do her best in life. Yet once again, I am struck down by something I never saw coming.

Honestly, it feels like if it weren't for my boys, then I wouldn't be able to go on sometimes.

But I do have my boys, and it's the thought of Noah and Oscar that makes me grit my teeth and put on a brave face.

I get into the car that will take me to my parents' house. This news will be deeply upsetting to the boys when they hear that their beloved bedrooms, toys and posters are no more, so I need to try to make this as easy for them as I can. What they won't need is seeing their mother so upset. I'll have to save my tears for in private, just like I did when Peter told me there was another woman. And just like I did when I found out his mistress took her own life because he chose me over her.

This really has been the year from hell.

But if there is one source of consolation in all of this, then surely it is that things can't get any worse.

Right?

33

EVE

It's an exciting day for me because I'm on my way to meet Karen for a coffee. It's been a while since the two of us got together for a catch-up, but that is understandable, considering how much Karen had to deal with lately. The fire was three weeks ago, and I have been enjoying reading all the social media gossip about it online.

Worried mums speculating on the internet, trying to find out if their families are also in danger from a crazy person or a faulty appliance.

How did the fire start?

Was it bad wiring due to the work of a dodgy electrician who might work in town?

Or was it arson?

But I didn't enjoy that half as much as when I saw the look on Karen's and Peter's faces after arriving home, when they got a first glimpse of the devastation the fire caused.

From my hiding place on the corner of their street, I watched their reactions as they spoke to several of the emergency service workers on-site. I wasn't able to hear what was being said, but that didn't dampen my feelings of pleasure from seeing the pair shake their heads, slouch their shoulders and stare dejectedly at their wrecked home.

Burning everything they owned was fun, but my vendetta against them is not ending there. I have much more in store for them, and as I walk into the coffee shop and see Karen sitting at the table, I can't wait to pile more misery onto her and her family.

It's clear from her pale complexion that Karen is not wearing makeup, just as it's clear from the bags under her eyes that she hasn't been sleeping well. But I'm not offended by her lack of effort in her appearance. If anything it only makes me even happier, because it shows how much she is struggling, and I can't wait to crack open that fragile mind of hers a little more.

I reach her table and open my arms to her.

'Karen! There you are! How are you doing, my love? Come here!'

I'm playing the part of 'extremely concerned friend' as well as I can. Karen gets up from her seat, and I embrace her.

'I'm so sorry about the fire. I'm just glad you and your family are okay. Tell me, how are you all getting on?'

We take our seats before Karen explains to me that things have been extremely difficult recently. She is sorry for not replying to a few of my messages over the last few weeks.

'Oh, don't worry about that. You've had so much on your plate,' I say.

The waiter comes over, and I order a latte from him.

I ask Karen if I can get her anything, but she just shakes her head and nurses the bottle of water she brought with her. I take it as a sign she is cutting her costs now that she lost everything she owns in the fire.

'I can't bring myself to go back there,' Karen says when I ask her if she's returned to the house since the night of the fire. 'Peter has been a couple of times with the police, but there isn't much to see. Everything's gone.'

'I'm so sorry,' I say again before digging into what the police know. 'Have they any idea what caused it yet?'

Karen just stares at the table. She answers, but when she does, it's apparent why she's taking her time before speaking.

'They say it was arson.'

'What?'

I hope my startled cry conveys the right amount of shock.

'They think somebody started it on purpose, possibly by pouring fuel through the letterbox.'

'You have got to be joking...'

Karen shakes her head slowly while I carry on pretending to be incredulous.

'Who the hell would do such a thing?' I ask, but thankfully, Karen has no answers there.

'I have no idea,' she mumbles. The waiter returns with my coffee. I thank him and give it a stir.

'Do the police have any leads?'

'No.'

'Maybe it wasn't arson. Maybe they're wrong.'

'They're not.' She sighs. 'It doesn't matter. The insurance company won't pay out while there's still an investigation underway, so we're screwed until then.'

'That's awful.'

'Tell me about it. We're staying with my parents now, but it's so cramped there, and it's not good for the boys to not have their own space. Oscar is acting up at school again, and Noah has been much quieter than usual since the fire. It's really taking a toll on them.'

'And on you, I imagine.'

'Yeah,' Karen mumbles before taking a sip from her water bottle.

'And what about Peter?' I ask, cradling my coffee cup and

enjoying the warmth from it. 'How's he been coping with all of this?'

'He's trying to get on with things, just like he always does. He's good at shutting things out. But it's not so good when I'm one of the things being shut out.'

'I'm sorry to hear that.'

'It's just my life,' Karen says with a simple shrug. 'Nothing's ever perfect, and when it is, it doesn't take long for something to mess it all up.'

'I'm sure things will get better,' I try to reassure her, but she doesn't seem so convinced.

'I don't know what to do. I'm so exhausted trying to keep my family happy while we're in someone else's house, and at the same time have to deal with fire reports and phone calls from police officers asking more questions. Then there's all the insurance paperwork, which is a nightmare. And of course, I'm still expected to keep going to work.'

'Won't they give you any time off?'

'Only if I take annual leave, which I don't have much of.'

It's my turn to shrug now; this interaction is looking like one big pity party. But then Karen asks me how I have been doing lately, so I make up some stuff about my personal life. Before long we reach the end of our time together, and Karen tells me she has to get back to her parents and make sure Peter hasn't murdered his in-laws.

We hug again outside the coffee shop. As I walk away from Karen, I feel like I'm ready to move forward with the next and last part of my plan. The fact that the police figured out the fire was arson was to be expected, but still adds a little more urgency to what I still need to do. I don't think I'm in any danger of getting caught before I finish – which is the most important thing – but I still need to make sure Karen and Peter don't suspect how their stay at Leanne's house played a part in what happened that night.

There's no way Karen would suspect. Why would she?

But Peter is different. He knows the holiday home wasn't just some random place he was staying in on the night his house burned down. Will he figure out that somebody is deliberately messing with him because of what he did in the past?

I am certain he will.

I just need to make sure he figures it out on *my* terms first.

34

PETER

'Oscar, put that down!'

I lunge at my son, who has just picked up an expensive-looking ornament of a church that Karen's parents keep on their mantelpiece. I manage to take it off him before he can cause any damage to it. But that's the third time that he has picked up the same ornament, and I know why he is doing it.

He's deliberately being mischievous because he wants attention. The reason he is craving that attention is because he is now in a house with more people than he is used to, and so that change of circumstance has led to a change of behaviour.

The more people there are means the bigger the audience for his childish games.

But I'm just about at the end of my tether with it now. I put the ornament back on the mantelpiece.

'Go upstairs!' I tell my six-year-old son, to prevent the breakage of something else in this house that doesn't belong to us. Oscar has already managed to snap a leg on one of the kitchen chairs because he was leaning back on it. That was not very helpful for Karen's parents, who are kindly letting us live here rent-free.

'You can't tell me what to do,' Oscar replies smugly. 'It's not your house.'

'Don't be cheeky with me, young man. Go upstairs. Now!'

I'm aware that my voice is loud and that hearing me so worked up is only likely to make everyone feel even more uncomfortable, but I can't help it. My youngest son is pushing all my buttons, and I've lost control of my emotions.

'No!' Oscar runs from the room. I'm not in the mood to let him get away with his misbehaviour that easily, so I chase my little boy through the hallway and into the kitchen, where his grandparents are trying to have a quiet cup of tea.

They stop what they are doing and watch Oscar running around them while I try to grab him. And even though they attempt to get their grandson to calm down too, it doesn't work. The disobedience continues, which means my bad mood continues as well.

'Get here now!' I say as I manage to get hold of his left arm and pull him towards me, but he wriggles away and runs from the room again, leaving me looking like more of a fool than when I first came in here.

It's only the sound of the front door opening that stops me from going fully ballistic with Oscar. Karen is back, and that means an extra pair of hands to help me around here.

My wife asks me what is going on when she notices my red face and my exasperated expression. After explaining to her that Oscar is being a nuisance again, she goes away to catch up with him and bring him back into line. While she does that, I go into the living room and take a seat on the sofa, mainly because this is the only room other than the bathroom that is not currently occupied by someone, and I just really want some space to myself.

I know it's kind of Karen's parents to have us here until

we get the insurance money for the house, because it's certainly a lot cheaper than us moving into a hotel. But it's wearing on me not having my own space, and I can tell that it's having the same effect on the rest of my family. Oscar is acting out, Noah is getting quieter by the day, and Karen and I stand no chance of mending our relationship while we are here.

We need our own place, and fast. But there is no end in sight, and that's because of the theory that the fire at our house was started deliberately.

Having initially presumed the fire was caused by faulty wiring or some other innocent reason, I was stunned to hear that we may have been targeted. Since then, I have been racking my brains to think of who would do such a despicable thing to me and my family. Of course, it could have been random, but I'm not sure how many people start fires in the homes of people they don't know. It makes more sense that the arsonist knew who lived in the house and that was why they poured petrol through the letterbox.

But who is that arsonist?

There are many reasons why I want to know the answer, least of which is that bringing them to justice would speed up our insurance claim. But I also want to know because if there really is someone out there targeting me and my family in a place we could easily have been in at the time, then I need to find out who they are before they strike again.

But the police have no leads. Not a single suspect. Nobody was seen at the property on the night of the fire. So where does that leave us? Clutching at straws. Or more specifically, it leaves us stuck in this house that isn't ours, getting grumpier and more frustrated by the day.

I should have savoured my rare moment of alone time a little more than I did because it's over again when Karen walks into the room. She slumps down next to me onto the sofa and lets out a deep breath before taking out her phone and handing it to me.

'I got this earlier,' she says. I look down at the email open on her device. 'It's from Sarah. The woman at the holiday home.'

Hi Karen. First of all, let me just say that I was terribly sorry to learn about the fire at your home. I read about it online recently. I hope you and your family are doing okay under these difficult circumstances. I was also wondering if I might be able to help a little. If you and your family would like a break, then you would be more than welcome to stay at the holiday home, free of charge of course. No problem if not, but I just thought you might need a break from everything. Let me know if so, and again, I hope you and your family are okay. Sarah.

Karen asks me what I think, but I read the message again before I answer.

'How does she know about the fire?' is my first question.

'My name was in that newspaper article. Remember?'

'I told you that you shouldn't have spoken to that journalist. Now everyone in town knows whose house it was that burnt down.'

'I know, but I thought they might be able to help.'

'No journalist can help us.'

'Whatever, that's not the point.' Karen sighs. 'Sarah invited us to a free stay at the holiday home. What do you think? I'd say we could use it right about now.'

My wife seems very sure, but I'm not so certain. I mean, there is no doubt we need a change of scene; the thought of escaping from my in-laws for a day or two is certainly appealing. But I'm not sure I want to 'escape' to that place again.

I feared at the time we stayed in the holiday home that it

also being Leanne's old house wasn't a coincidence. Since then however, I have no other evidence to fuel my concerns. The fire happening on that exact same night could be just a coincidence too. But now we're being invited back, I'm starting to wonder if this invitation isn't too good to be true.

'I don't know,' I say. 'How about we go somewhere else?'

'Where else can we go for free?' Karen asks me as she takes back her phone. 'I don't know if you've noticed, but we're not exactly flush with cash right now, what with all our things having been burnt to bits and all.'

'There's no need to be sarcastic.'

'And there's no need to look a gift horse in the mouth. Sarah is being extremely kind, so I don't see what the problem is.'

'But why is she being kind to us? Have you asked yourself that?'

'What do you mean?'

'I mean this woman is a stranger. She seems to be going out of her way to get us back to that house. Why is that?'

'Because she read about the fire in the newspaper and is trying to be nice!'

'Is she?'

'What else would she be doing?'

I sigh. 'I don't know. All I do know is that the fire happened on the same night we were at her house, and now she wants us to go back.'

Karen gives me an incredulous look. 'You think she had something to do with the fire?'

'I don't know. Maybe.'

'Don't be ridiculous!'

'Am I though?'

'Yes, of course you are! Why would you think that Sarah had anything to do with what happened?'

'I don't know.'

'Exactly. Because it's nonsense!'

Karen throws up her arms, clearly exasperated with me and this conversation, and while it is a familiar reaction from her these days, what isn't familiar is the sense of dread I feel in my stomach.

'How well do you know this Sarah?' I ask my wife. 'I mean you've never met her, right?'

'That's right.'

'So how do we know she is genuine?'

'What do you mean?'

'What if she's playing games with us?'

'What on earth are you talking about now?'

I come very close then to telling Karen that Sarah's home used to belong to Leanne, but I catch myself, still too afraid of mentioning my mistress's name and churning up old feelings. But if I don't tell her, how can I explain myself?

Karen is staring at me, still waiting for some kind of logical answer, but I am a coward. I can't tell her *how* I have a history with that house. Because of that, my wife sees no reason why we can't accept the invitation to the holiday home.

'The boys need a break from here,' she says, typing out a reply to Sarah's email. 'And my parents need a break from us too. I'll see when we can go. The four of us. After what we have all been through, it's about time we had something go our way for once.'

I grit my teeth while Karen lets Sarah know we are interested in a free stay, but as I do, I also see an opportunity. Going back there might be the only chance I have of getting to the bottom of any possible coincidences. The police have no idea who targeted our house, and I'm not sure they ever will, at least not unless the person who committed that crime is coaxed out into the open again. If this Sarah is up to something, then going back there might be the only way to find out what it is.

It's risky, but then so is carrying on with our lives knowing that somebody out there wants to hurt us. The paranoia of knowing they could strike at any time overwhelms me daily.

At least this way, if the holiday home is linked to everything else that happened, I've got a chance of finding out why.

And more importantly, who is behind it all.

35

Walking through the front door of the holiday home for the third time, I'm not expecting this visit to be as relaxing as the first one was or the second one should have been. On both occasions, I was either alone or with Peter, but now I have my kids in tow, and there's never much relaxing when that is the case. But we're here as a unit because we all deserve a change of scenery, just like my beleaguered parents deserve to have their house to themselves for one night before we return and take it over again.

Noah and Oscar have already run off to explore their new surroundings. Peter and I put our bags down in the hallway, happy to let them entertain themselves as long as they don't touch anything or, more importantly, break anything.

I go upstairs to do a little unpacking while a moping Peter goes to check on the boys. I am aware that my husband hardly said a word since we left my mum and dad's place. Now that we're here, I'm hoping he will start to unwind a little.

I admire the view from the bedroom window as I unpack

our suitcase, feeling lucky to be here, given all the other unlucky things that happened so far. Not everything in life is bad, and this scenery is a reminder of that fact.

Peter cries out from downstairs. The sound sends me scampering out of the bedroom to check that everything is okay. I find him in the kitchen and see what caused him to shout. Noah and Oscar were obviously raiding the cupboards, possibly looking for something to eat, and despite being here only a few minutes, they managed to make quite the mess.

I do my best to get the kitchen back to some semblance of order, leaving Peter to tell our sons that they need to calm down. He suggests they check out the movie room in the basement. It seems like that is a good idea, because the boys run out of the kitchen. I hear their little feet padding down the steps that will take them below the house.

'Don't shut the door!' I call out to them, remembering the latch on it and fearing a repeat of my children locking themselves in yet another room. But they do as they are told, and I can rest easy – for one minute at least.

It's nice to have some quiet again, but soon I'm concerned with how quiet it is. I tell Peter to go down there, make sure they aren't making a mess. But he seems reluctant to go, instead preferring to stand by the window and look out of it. I get that it's a lovely view, but I just asked him to do something, so why is he ignoring me?

'Peter,' I say, snapping him out of his trance.

'Sorry,' he mumbles before he does as I say.

My husband's quiet behaviour continues to puzzle me, but before I have time to worry about it, I hear the beep from my mobile phone that tells me I have a new message.

When I check it, I see it's from Sarah.

Hi Karen. I hope you managed to get in okay and are

*having a good time. Just wondered if you could leave me
a review again? I'm finally getting around to making a
website, and I'm going to use some of the reviews on
there for the homepage. I've got a new review book now.
You'll find it in the cupboard above the fridge. Thank you,
and have a fun time with your family!*

I look at the table where the old review book used to be. I
go to the new location Sarah says it's in and take it out, and
while I'm not planning on writing one now, I leave it out so I
don't forget to do it before we go.

But before I put it down again, I flick it open to see how
many reviews Sarah got since my stay. When I do, I get a
shock. I see something that should not be in any review book.

I see a photo.

Of me.

I stare at my image stuck to the open page, trying to think
of any reason why it would be in here. But it's not just the
presence of the picture that concerns me the most. It's where
it was taken. I'm standing outside Noah and Oscar's school,
alongside a couple of the other parents. Whoever took this
photo did so secretly, from a distance, without me having any
idea that they were there.

Who the hell would do that?

Sarah.

It has to be her. Who else? This is her home. Not only
that, but she messaged me about the review book. It is the
only reason I'm holding it right now. She must have wanted
me to see it.

But why?

What the hell is going on?

I turn the page in the review book – or what is supposed
to be the review book anyway –suddenly worried about what
else I might find in here. My heart races when I see more

photos, but these aren't of me this time. They are of Peter and the kids, taken from a distance again and in various locations.

Outside Peter's office. Outside the school. *Outside our house.*

It's clear that Sarah has been watching us for some time, unknown to any of us. I turn several more pages, and this is where the photos stop and the writing starts. But these aren't reviews. These are short, sharp sentences that send chills down my spine.

Your husband is a cheat.

You are so gullible.

The fire was not an accident.

You will pay for what you have done.

The pages are literally shaking as my hand trembles. I try to figure out what is happening, but I can't do it by myself. I need Peter now.

Rushing down to the basement with the book, I find my husband sat on the sofa, watching an action movie with our sons. But movie time is over – at least for him.

'We need to talk,' I tell Peter sternly. 'Now.'

He can see that something is wrong, so he doesn't protest. Instead he untangles himself from Noah's and Oscar's limbs, who are stretched out across him, and gets up. He follows me out of the room and up the stairs.

I'm planning on showing Peter everything in the book and asking him if he has any idea what is going on. But unlike in the past, when he often tried to play dumb, I am expecting answers this time. That's because it's painfully obvious from the *your husband is a cheat* comment that everything that has happened so far, and continues to happen, has everything to do with his affair.

The door at the top of the basement stairs suddenly slams shut. I freeze in place when I hear a latch being put in place.

'Hey!' I cry out and rush up the last couple of steps, to get to the door as quickly as I can. But when I reach it, it won't open. 'Someone just locked us in!'

Peter joins me and tries to open it. But we soon realise this door doesn't open outwards.

'Who are you? What are you doing?' Peter cries out, hammering his fists on the door, shouting out to whoever is on the other side. But we get no response.

Noah and Oscar are at the bottom of the stairs, seeing what all the commotion is.

'We're trapped,' I say quietly to Peter, so the boys don't hear and get even more alarmed.

'Yeah,' he says with a solemn shake of the head. 'The question is why.'

36

EVE

Karen and Peter can bang on the door and demand they be let out all they want, but it doesn't matter. I'm not opening it. That will be a job for the emergency service workers when they eventually get here. By then, it will be too late.

I walk away from the locked basement door and return to the garage. It's where I left the jerrycan used successfully to burn down the first house. Now it's time to burn down my second house, only this time it won't just be damage to property that will occur. There will also be loss of life, and this fire won't just make the local headlines.

I made sure to refill the jerrycan with fuel before today. The flammable liquid sploshes around in the container as I walk it back into the house. I hear Karen crying out again for somebody to open this door, but I ignore her, just like I ignore the heavy banging that follows her demand. My prisoners are entitled to make as much noise as they want. After I'm done, it won't make any difference. They aren't getting out of this. The same might be said for me in the long run, but today, I don't care.

I'm not doing this for me.

I'm doing it for Leanne.

I just hope she is looking down and ready to enjoy the show.

I start pouring the petrol in the bedrooms, splashing a healthy amount of the liquid over all the beds, before trailing it along the carpet in the upstairs landing and down the stairs. Then I splash more onto the curtains, walls and the sofa in the living room before making sure the kitchen gets a good coating too. I finish by emptying the remainder of the petrol on and around the locked basement door, making sure that this will be a hotspot once the fire begins in a few moments' time.

I toss the jerrycan aside – because I know I won't need it again – and go into the kitchen to find the box of matches I stored in there after the first fire. The police suspected arson then, but in this case, the reason will be as obvious as a sunrise. It will also be obvious that the poor family who perished in this fire were trapped here deliberately, and while that might seem like a heinous crime to an outside observer, I will know my actions were fully justified.

Peter took a life with his actions; it's only fair that I take his life in return.

He could have left Karen. He could have kept his word and started a new life with Leanne, just as he promised her he would. While I would have secretly resented him for getting to be with Leanne, I would have coped because at least Leanne would have been happy. She would still be here for me to chat to, whether over the phone or in person. We would still be in each other's lives, sharing our news and laughing as we reminisced about the old times. But Peter robbed me of that future with Leanne when he backtracked on his promise and went back to his wife. That's why he deserves to die now. Not only that, but he also deserves to know what it feels like to lose a loved one, just like I do. He will learn all about that while he watches his family die alongside him.

I'm aware that I am punishing Karen, too, and her children. I'm using the kids to increase Peter's suffering, but I also have the desire to make Karen suffer a little too.

I hate her almost as much as Peter, simply for the fact that she could have ended that sham of a marriage. She didn't have to take her cheating husband back, even if that was what he wanted. She could have kicked him to the kerb. If she had done that, then maybe Peter would have returned to Leanne – even if it was for lack of a better option. If that had happened, my dear friend would not have taken her life. But no, Karen is just as selfish as Peter, choosing to preserve her imperfect lifestyle, playing it safe rather than admit her relationship is doomed and move on with her life.

Everyone moves on from heartbreak, except Karen and Peter didn't. After his affair came to light, they went backwards, and in the process they completely destroyed Leanne. That beautiful, gentle soul who just wanted to be loved.

'I'm so sorry this happened to you,' I say out loud as I look around at the petrol-soaked furniture and feel the scent of it tickling my nostrils. 'I'm so sorry they did this to you. But I'm putting it right. It'll be over soon. I promise.'

Talking out loud to my dead friend in an empty room isn't the same as having her right here with me, but it's all I have. I walk to the bottom of the stairs with the matches rattling inside the box I hold. I wonder if my prisoners in the basement smell the fuel yet and have some idea of the fate that is about to befall them. I hope so, because that will only increase their fear and panic. But if they haven't smelt the petrol yet, then it's only a matter of time before they smell the smoke.

Carefully lighting the match that will see this beautiful

home reduced to nothing but ashes, I stare at the flickering flame for a brief moment, in awe of its beauty as well as the sheer, destructive power it possesses. But fire is only useful if it has something to burn, and that's why I turn this small flame into a much larger one when I toss the match onto the line of petrol running all the way up the staircase carpet.

A bright, orange streak suddenly explodes into life when the fuel ignites. The fire races along the line of petrol, all the way up and into the bedrooms above. I allow the blaze to heat my skin for a moment before common sense kicks in, and I retreat before the fire really takes hold.

As I rush to the front door, I take a moment to look back, aware that this will be the last time I ever see this house, experience all the memories that its four walls hold. Leanne and I had so many good times here. But there were many bad ones too.

I'll never forget the night I held her as she cried and trembled in my arms, telling me that Peter broke her heart and she couldn't bear the pain of living. The anger I felt burning inside me that night could easily match the strength of the fire burning on the floor above me. But it was nothing compared to when I found out Leanne was serious about not being able to go on and she killed herself over a broken heart.

It's only right that Peter and his family reach their demise here.

And it's only right that this place will be rebuilt, because it's time for a fresh start, and that's only possible by completely erasing the past.

I close the front door and walk away, striding defiantly down the driveway, to a safe distance where I can watch the house burn. But I'm not smirking as I go, nor am I feeling particularly excited inside. This is still a sad ending to a heartbreaking story, whichever way I look at it.

Just because I got my revenge doesn't mean that any of

this had to happen. This could have all been easily avoided. Leanne could have found a single man instead of a married one. Peter could have remained faithful to his wife instead of cheating. And Karen could have ended it all a year ago instead of dragging it out and continuing to play happy families when she was far from happy.

Well, there is nothing happy about that family anymore, that's for certain. I get confirmation of that when I check the basement camera on my phone and see my four prisoners panicking as their situation goes from bad to worse.

37

KAREN

'Damn it, there's no signal down here!' I cry after confirming my mobile phone is indeed useless.

I get Peter to check his device, just in case we get lucky, but we don't, and his can't be used to call for help either.

'I told you there was something suspicious about Sarah,' my husband says, almost blaming me for the mess we find ourselves in. He quickly apologises because he knows better than to start an argument now when tempers are already frayed.

We need to stay composed, not only to give us the best chance of figuring a way out, but also to keep the two boys calm, who are standing behind us and looking very worried.

'Why are we locked in?' Oscar wants to know, and even though he is now very still and quiet, I long for the times when he is louder and wilder, because that would tell me he was at least being himself. Seeing him calm only proves how scared he is about this situation.

Noah is standing beside his younger brother, and he looks

just as pensive, which only fuels my desire to get us out of this basement as quickly as possible. But how can we do that?

'There has to be another way out of here,' Peter says, rushing back down the steps and forcing our sons out of the way so their dad can get into the movie room again. But I know there isn't.

There are no windows or doors except for one. That's what makes it a great place to watch films. It is dark. Private. Secure.

I call after Peter to tell him not to waste his time looking, but he doesn't listen. I'm sure in his mind trying something that probably won't work is better than to keep trying something that definitely isn't working. And we already proved that banging on this locked door and calling for it to be opened is not.

I wonder if the person who is doing this to us is just trying to scare us. It's bad, but it might not get any worse than this. Of course, I'll still be furious when I finally get out of here, but it wouldn't be the end of the world if I didn't learn who is doing this. As long as my family is safe. As frightened as they are right now, they are still that. We all are.

After another couple of hits on the door, I decide I have wasted enough of my rapidly depleting energy. I look down and see the 'review book' lying on the ground. I must have dropped it when I scrambled up here to get to this door before it locked. But I pick it up again now and look inside, wondering if it might hold any clues as to who is doing this and, more importantly, how we can get out of here.

But after flicking through the same pictures of me and my family, I feel like there is nothing more to learn from this book. But that's where I'm wrong, because then I notice a couple of new images that I didn't see the first time. I inspect them closer and recognise the room they were taken in.

It's my living room at home, or at least it was my living room before it was destroyed.

I recognise the sofa, the coffee table and the photo on the wall. What I don't recognise are the feet propped up on my coffee table, making it look like whoever took this picture was in a reclined and relaxed position when they did so.

'Nope. There's no other bloody way out of here,' Peter moans as he returns to the stairs, only proving what I already told him.

But in this moment, there's something else on my mind.

'Who is this?' I ask him, holding out the page with the photo stuck to it.

He comes closer, as do Noah and Oscar, but I hold the book up high so only their father can get a good look at it.

'Who is that?' I say, referring to the person in our living room. 'When was this taken?'

Peter looks confused as he studies the photo before shrugging and saying he has no idea.

'You must do. This photo was taken in our house!'

'Was it?'

'Yes, that's our living room. Don't play dumb. You know it is!'

'Okay, so it's in our house. That doesn't mean I know *who* it is.'

'Is it another woman?'

'What?'

'Did you have another woman in our house?'

I know I shouldn't be having this discussion with Peter in front of the kids, because I'm not sure where it might lead, but I have to know.

'No!'

'Those are women's feet. So who is she?'

'I don't know. I swear!'

'Liar.'

I throw the book at Peter; the frustration of this situation is getting to me. I watch the book bounce off him and tumble down the stairs before it lands at Noah's feet.

When he picks it up, I rush down the stairs towards him, before he can read any of the nasty things that are written in there, as well as see the secret photos of him and his brother outside their school. But he gets the book before I do and looks at the photo of the woman's feet.

What he says next surprises me.

'Is this the woman who came to our house when Mum was out?'

I realise the question is directed at Peter. I turn to my husband, eager to hear what his answer might be.

'What?' he asks Noah.

'That woman who came. Remember? She said she was a new neighbour.'

Peter furrows his brow, as if he's trying to work something out. I turn back to my eldest son, because it seems like he has more information than my husband at present.

'What woman? What new neighbour?'

'I don't want to get in trouble,' he says quickly, and tries to hand me back the book.

But it's too late for that.

'What are you talking about?' I demand. 'Tell me now!'

Noah looks at his little brother rather sheepishly, perhaps because he realises he made a mistake in opening his mouth. I urge him again to tell me before he locks away whatever secret he has.

'It was the night you went away on holiday by yourself,' Noah says quietly. 'I snuck out of bed because I couldn't sleep and was playing with my toys when I heard the front door. I crept to the top of the stairs and looked down and saw Daddy talking to a woman.'

'Who was she?'

'I don't know, but she came in. And she had a bottle of wine.'

It feels as though my heart is being ripped in two all over again, just like it was last year. I listen to my son tell me about the mystery woman my husband had in my house while I was away.

I'm seething, and not just because this information came from Noah, but because it seems to prove to me what I feared all along. Peter hasn't changed. He's still making the same mistakes, and he's still walking all over me.

But that stops right now.

I turn to my husband, red-faced and ready for a war, but he holds out his hands, in his best attempt to calm me down.

'Nothing happened, I swear.'

'Why didn't you tell me about her, then? Why do I have to hear this from Noah?'

'I didn't want you to think anything was going on.'

'So you decided the best way to do that was to keep secrets from me? Again!'

I really wish my kids weren't here, because I would love nothing more than to unleash all of my fury upon my lying husband, but their presence is enough to keep me somewhat restrained.

'What's her name?' I ask, not that it would make it alright.

'Erm, I don't know. Natasha, I think.'

'Don't act like she's some stranger. She's been in our house!'

'But nothing happened.'

'What if she's the one doing this?' Noah suddenly asks, and that brings a halt to the escalating argument. 'What if she's the one who locked us in?'

'Don't be silly,' Peter says, but I don't dismiss the suggestion so easily.

'Could it be her?' I ask him.

'No, of course not. This is Sarah, can't you see? She's the one who owns this place.'

'But I've never met her. Sarah could just be a name. Just like Natasha.'

Peter scoffs but then has pause for thought, because he knows I could be right.

'How did you meet her?' I ask him.

'She turned up at the house.'

'When?'

'On the first night you went away.'

The look we give each other confirms that we both think it to be extremely suspect in hindsight.

'Was that the night she came into the house?' I ask.

'No, it was the next night. The second night you were away. I'd bumped into her at the school when I was picking up the boys earlier that day. She invited herself in, I swear.'

'But I came home early that second night. Why didn't I see her?'

Peter pauses before answering, then admits that he sent her out the back door.

I shake my head at his confession, but there will be time to discuss it at a later date. Right now, we need to figure out who this woman really is.

'So if this Sarah or Natasha – or whatever she is called – is doing all this, then we need to know why.'

'It doesn't matter why; we just need to get out,' Peter says, climbing the stairs and trying the handle again.

'It has to do with what you did,' I say to him, being careful to keep what he *did* vague so that the boys don't understand. 'So think. How could she be connected to *her*?'

I still can't bring myself to say Leanne's name, but Peter gets who I mean. He turns back to me, letting go of the handle because the door still won't open.

'Wait, how did you find out about this house in the first place?' Peter asks me.

'I told you. A friend recommended it,' I reply.

And then it dawns on me. How I might have been set up. How I might have been betrayed by someone else other than my husband.

'Eve,' I mumble, wondering if it could be true.

Could the woman I thought was my friend be the one who brought us all here to suffer?

'I never met her,' Peter says solemnly, adding more weight to the idea that this woman could have deceived us both. She might have introduced herself differently when she met us separately.

'No, it can't be her,' I say, shaking my head. 'I know her. We're friends.'

'You met her in the gym, right? She came up to you? Started talking to you? Just like Natasha came to me?'

I nod. It does seem plausible. It really could be her.

Eve. Sarah. Natasha. *Are they all the same woman?*

But if that realisation wasn't bad enough, what happens next is.

'Mum, I can smell something burning,' Oscar says, rubbing his nose.

Then Noah points to the door, and when Peter and I look up, we see smoke coming in underneath it.

38

The panic from my prisoners tells me that they've realised the house is on fire and they no longer have time to stand around and discuss their predicament.

I'm enjoying watching them squirm on camera, and I wish Leanne were here to watch it with me. The best I can do is hold the photo of my late friend in my hand and look up at the flames licking at the windows, as well as watch the smoke billowing out from the roof.

Even at this safe distance, I can feel some of the heat from the fire, so I can only imagine how hot it is getting in that basement. I suspect the four family members are sweating badly while their fight for survival becomes more urgent by the second. But out here in the cool fresh air, I am feeling very good about things. I know I'll have to leave shortly, before the fire engines arrive and the police officers cordon this place off, but I think I still have a few more minutes to enjoy the fruits of my labour. Or at least I did until I hear the sound of a car behind me screeching into the driveway.

I recognise the vehicle immediately. While it's a relief to

learn the car doesn't belong to emergency services, it's still a problem to see it here. That's because it's being driven by Colin and Pam, Leanne's parents and the owners of the house that is burning right behind me.

The pair spot me crouching behind bushes.

'Oh my God!' Colin cries as he gets out of the car. 'The whole thing's going up!'

'Are you okay?' Pam asks as she rushes over, putting my personal well-being above the property burning nearby.

'Yeah, I'm okay,' I say, doing my best to act a little shaken up. I pretend as if I'm stunned by both the fire and the fact that I managed to get out unharmed.

'What the hell happened?' Colin wants to know. 'How did it start?'

'I don't know,' I reply with a shake of the head. 'I just saw the flames and ran for it.'

'Have you called 999?' he asks me as he looks at the house. His eyes are lit up by the brightness of the fire.

'Of course I have,' I tell him, even though it's a blatant lie, but then I see Colin take out his phone and start dialling anyway.

'What are you doing? I told you I called them,' I tell him, hoping he will put his phone away and delay the real call for help even more.

'Well, they need to be quicker, because this whole place is going to be gone in a minute!'

His call connects, and he barks down the phone at the operator, telling them that he needs the fire brigade and he needs it now.

'It's going to be okay,' Pam says, putting her arm around me. 'I know it was Leanne's place, but it's only a house. We'll still have all the memories.'

'Yeah, I suppose,' I say, shrugging, as if I'm devastated to see this place burning. But I'm not. If anything, I wish it were burning quicker, because now that Colin has called for help, it won't be long before dozens of firefighters arrive here.

But then I wonder something. How did Colin and Pam know to come here when they did? It can't be a coincidence that they just happened to visit moments after a fire breaks out. Karen and Peter might believe in coincidences, but I don't. I know that everything in life happens as a direct result of cause and effect. So what happened?

'Why are you here?' I ask Pam. Colin paces in front of us, hands on his head.

'We got a call from one of the neighbours saying they saw smoke, and they thought it was coming from Leanne's place,' Pam tells me. 'They said they called 999, but they wanted to let us know too.'

Colin and Pam only live five minutes away from here, so it makes sense that a neighbour might alert them to this. But it troubles me that the same neighbour also alerted the emergency services a while ago, because that means they should be a lot closer than I expect.

Sure enough, I hear sirens a second later, and now I start to worry that there might be a chance the firefighters could douse the flames enough to give those trapped in the basement a fighting chance.

I want to check on the camera and see how Karen and her family are getting on, but I can't do that with Pam standing as close to me as she is, still with her arm around me, acting like a concerned parent. I always got on well with her parents, and in particular Pam, who was like a mother to me. But their presence is more of a hindrance than a help, and not just because I can't savour this moment with them here.

It's because it's going to make it harder for me to disappear before the authorities arrive.

'We can't just stand here and do nothing,' Colin suddenly says. 'We have to try something.'

With that, he rushes towards the side of the house and turns on the garden tap before looking around for something to fill.

'Don't be stupid. Get away from there!' Pam rather wisely tells him, and she rushes after him to make sure he doesn't get any closer to the danger.

Colin resists at first, so Pam asks me to help her, but I just stay where I am, frustrated by their fretting that is ruining what is supposed to be an enjoyable time for me.

But Pam eventually makes her husband see sense and leads him back down the driveway, away from the fire. But he's still not happy about things, and he declares as much by telling us he can't stand and watch this. He turns away from the house and looks towards the front of the property.

That's when he notices something.

'Where's the For Sale sign?' he asks me, breaking my concentration on the inferno raging through the window of what used to be the living room.

'What?' I mumble, keeping my eyes on the fire.

'The For Sale sign,' he repeats. 'It's not there. Where is it?'

'I don't know.'

'It doesn't matter,' Pam tells her husband, but he isn't having it.

'Did you take it down?' Colin presses. 'Is this why this place hasn't been selling? And is this why the estate agent told us this morning that you cancelled the last two viewings?'

'This isn't the time,' Pam tries again, but Colin is like a dog with a bone.

'You've been sabotaging the sale of this place, haven't you?' he says before a look of horror comes over his face. 'Oh my God, did you start this fire too?'

I should probably deny that quickly, feigning ignorance or being horrified at his suggestion, but I don't. I'm past the point of pretending with these two anymore. That's why I just stand there and watch the flames grow higher while the sirens get nearer.

'Colin, don't be ridiculous. Of course she didn't start this fire,' Pam cries, admonishing her husband for what she believes to be a crazy statement.

He's not having any of it.

'Look at her! Look how calm she is. She doesn't look like somebody who just escaped from a burning building.'

Colin makes a good point there. Now would also be a good time for me to get the hell out of here before it's too late. That's why I turn and start walking down the long driveway, but before I get to the path, the first fire engine arrives.

'Damn it,' I say under my breath. I stop and turn back to Colin and Pam and the burning house.

I guess I'll have to stick around, for now anyway.

As I watch the firefighters uncoil their hoses and drag them towards the flames, I console myself with the knowledge that at least I can guarantee nobody makes it out of here alive.

I'll keep watching the doors and windows, and every second that passes without seeing somebody exit will make me the happiest I have felt in a long time.

39

PETER

As the heat continues to build in the basement, I remove my sweater and stuff it along the bottom of the door to stop more smoke from getting into the room. Karen has taken the kids away from the locked door and farther into the basement, but that's only a short-term fix to keep them safe. With no way out and the house burning above us, it's only a matter of time before the fire gets in.

I rush back into the movie room and see the film that I was watching with my sons earlier is still playing. It's hard to believe everything was okay only a few minutes ago, when we were lying on the sofa and being entertained by the actors on-screen, but things have gone wrong very fast since then.

I try one more time to find another way out of this place, even though my first search proved fruitless. But my efforts only waste precious time, and soon I feel the beads of sweat running down my forehead, not only because of my effort, but also because of the heat from the inferno that is raging above our heads.

'Damn it!' I say when I fail to find another way out of here. I look over at Karen, who is sitting with Noah and Oscar and trying to keep them calm. But Oscar gets up suddenly and runs to the locked door. I rush after him to get him away from it again.

'Don't touch that handle! You'll burn yourself!' I tell my son, pulling him away before he can do himself harm.

'It's like when I get locked in the bathroom,' he tells me. 'Why don't you just take the door off?'

I stare at my son for a moment. The realisation of what he says hits me as our only real chance of getting out of here. Maybe I could take this door off. I did it plenty of times at home. But unlike those times, I don't have my tools.

'I can't do it without my screwdriver,' I say to Oscar despondently.

'Try, Daddy!' he urges me. Even with all the best will in the world, I know I won't be able to take this door off its hinges without that tool.

But I tell my son to step back because I feel like I should try, preferring to go down with a fight instead of passively waiting for this fire to consume us.

I run towards the door and slam my shoulder into it. Again. Again. *And again.*

I'm covered in sweat, and as I predicted, I'm getting nowhere. I can't barge this door open.

'Come on!' I cry, as if speaking to some guardian angel who might be watching. An angel that might hear me and help us before we burn to death. But even if there is some higher power listening right now, I get no response. I've not spoken to a higher power before, so maybe that's why.

I'm on my own with this one.

Or at least I am unless I sit with my family and spend these last few precious moments with them.

Returning to the movie room an exhausted and defeated man, I shake my head solemnly at my wife to let her know that it's no good. Then I take a seat beside her and look at my sons. Noah has tears in his eyes while Oscar is watching the movie on-screen. Maybe he is trying to distract himself because maybe it won't be real if he pretends everything is okay.

'I love you guys,' I say to them, and they say it back. Karen begins to sob, and even though I try to console her, the severity of the situation means she can't stop.

I decide we need a distraction in these last few moments, so I take out my wallet and remove the photo of us that I keep in there. It's the one of me and Karen with the boys in Greece, a couple of years ago. We asked one of the waiters in the hotel restaurant to take our picture. He got a good one, capturing us looking tanned and healthy, dressed in our good clothes as we prepared to tuck into a tasty meal.

'Remember this holiday?' I ask my sons. They look at the photo in my hand before nodding.

'I want to go back there,' Noah says suddenly.

I want to tell him that I can make that happen but I'm not sure I can, so I just smile and keep staring at the happy faces in the photo.

It's not at all tatty – amazing considering I've been carrying it around in my wallet for the last two years. As I look at my wallet, I see all the other things in there. Credit cards. A business card for the local dry-cleaner. And a ten-pound note that I'll never get to spend now.

The credit cards.

Taking one of the shiny pieces of plastic out, I inspect it while wondering if it might do what I need it to. Could I slide it between the door and the frame and potentially shimmy the latch on the other side? I've seen it done in films before, but that doesn't mean it works. It's also why I took the door off its hinges at home. It was messier, but it got quicker results.

But for the lack of a better option, I decide to go with the credit card. I head back to the door, telling my family to stay put, because the heat and smoke is getting worse.

The door is so hot now that I have to cover my hand with my sleeve. I attempt to slot the card into the gap in the doorframe. Then I move it slowly up and down, hoping to meet a little resistance in the general area where the latch should be, and hopefully lifting it up and unlocking this door so we can get out. I dread to think what horrors might be waiting for us on the other side, but getting the chance to see will mean we have half a chance of escaping. I pray this will work.

But it's not easy to keep the credit card steady and in place whilst standing beside a boiling-hot door. The smoke is seeping underneath it, and it's clear that the clothes I stuffed at the bottom of the door are no longer able to keep it out. But it's the thought of my wife and kids choking on those fumes that pushes me to keep trying. I stare at the edge of the card in my hand, the rest of it inside the doorframe, searching for that latch.

And then I feel something.

I presume it's the latch because it's in the centre of the doorframe, and when I try to move the credit card up, it no longer budges. This must be it. Now I just need to apply enough force to lift that stiff latch and get us out of here.

The feeling of relief that washes over me when the latch moves overwhelms me, but it's also short-lived, because no sooner have I opened the door than I see the next obstacle in our way out.

A wall of flames licking at the walls. A black, heavy plume of smoke making it almost impossible to see.

My throat and nostrils burn from the acrid stench. I turn back and call to my family to come as quickly as they can. Oscar cheers when he sees I managed to get the door open, but any excitement soon fades when they see what they have to go through next.

'Oh my God,' Karen says, holding the hands of the two boys and staring at the fire behind me.

'Come on, we have to go now,' I say. 'I'll take Noah. You take Oscar. And, boys, do not let go under any circumstances, you hear me?'

Noah and Oscar nod, aware that this is no time for defiance. If this weren't such a precarious situation, I'd enjoy the feeling of having them do what I ask without complaining.

'Okay, use the collar of your tops to cover your mouths,' I tell them, demonstrating with mine. 'And whatever you do, don't stop. Keep going until you get out of here. You understand?'

I'm talking more to Karen now, because while I know I will keep pushing forward with Noah, I have to know she will do the same thing with Oscar, whatever happens. The way I see it, any of us will be lucky to get out of here alive, so I don't want one party stopping if they see the other is in difficulty. That could spell doom for all of us.

'I love you guys,' I say, smiling at my boys, then looking at Karen. 'And I love you, you know that.'

Karen nods and grips Oscar's hand more tightly, showing she is ready to do what is necessary.

'Okay, let's get out of here.'

I push forward, Noah beside me, our mouths covered, our bloodshot eyes squinting and straining to see the exit routes amid the orange flames and suffocating smoke. But my intimate knowledge of this place gives me a better chance at navigating my way out. I'm able to get us into the living room relatively quickly, even though I can barely see what's in front of me. At this point, I'm just trying not to succumb to smoke inhalation before we make it to the front door, but every second we spend in here gives the flames a chance to grow bigger. Soon they will block every exit route, so there's no time to waste.

'This way!' I call out after a brief moment to pause and recalibrate. I'm not sure Karen and Oscar hear my cry, because the noise from the raging fire is deafening, but I try anyway. As long as they can still see me, then that's all that matters. And a quick glance back confirms they are still on my tail.

When we reach the hallway, I hear a loud groan right before the staircase collapses. The centre of it caves in on itself, consumed by the fire, rendering another part of the house entirely inaccessible now. But we don't need to go up. We're all down here, so we still have a chance, or at least I think we do until I look at the front door, or at least where it should be.

All I see is a wall of orange.

The fire is blocking our best escape route.

'Damn it!' I cry, squeezing Noah's hand tightly to make sure he knows to stop too.

Glancing around, I look for the second best way out of here. We're going to have to backtrack.

Passing the crippled staircase, we re-enter the living room. I look over at the patio doors, beyond which is that spectacular view, and it's the thought of breathing in all that fresh air that drives me forward. I lead my eldest son past a burning sofa and towards the doors.

I reach them, but even though they are locked, I don't let that stop me. Warning my son to turn away and cover his eyes, I kick through the glass door, shattering it. The glass cuts me in the process, but the gust of cool air that flows in makes any pain worth it.

Leading Noah outside, a feeling of unbridled joy washes over me. We both suck in a lungful of clean air and cough; the fire is no longer overwhelming, but the smoke is still in our lungs. It's almost a funny juxtaposition to go from being in a burning house seconds ago to looking down over the fields full of sheep.

Almost funny.

'Are you okay?' I ask my son. I check him over for visible signs of injury or distress.

But he seems fine, or as fine as any eight-year-old who just survived a house fire would be.

With Noah okay, I turn around to check on my wife and other son, hoping they are just as unscathed. But I can't see them.

Karen and Oscar aren't here.

40

KAREN

'Help me, Mummy!' Oscar cries as he continues to tug on his leg. It went through a weakened floorboard while we were following Peter and Noah. As hard as I try, I can't help him free his trapped limb.

I saw which way Peter went and called out to him as loudly as I could, but he didn't hear us. Instead, he made it through the patio doors, and now he is outside with Noah. I'm thrilled, but it also means he's not here to help us.

Oscar screams when I keep tugging at his trapped leg. There's no way I will leave my son here in this burning hellhole, so I crouch down and take hold of his leg again before pulling as hard as I can. My son howls in pain as I try to free him, and I worry that his leg could be broken, but right now, we just have to get out of here by whatever means possible.

Broken bones can heal.

Death is permanent.

Oscar cries out again when I keep pulling. I glance over at the broken patio doors, wondering if I will be able to see Peter coming back to help us. But I can't see him yet through the smoke. Maybe that's for the best. At least he made it out with Noah. Perhaps it's better if they stay clear of this place now so we're not all lost in this fire.

My eyes are streaming, but it's not just from the smoke. I'm crying because I'm so afraid that I won't be able to save my son. He's only six; he has such a long time ahead of him, and he has a full life to lead. But not if I can't get him out of here. Things will be over very soon if we can't escape.

Pulling with all my strength, I ignore Oscar's screams. Then a miracle happens. His leg is free, and he almost topples backwards from the jolt, but I catch his hand before he falls into the flames. Then I pull him towards me and hold him tightly, squeezing him to let him know he is okay and that I will never let go of him, no matter what happens next.

Then I pull him towards the patio doors, sensing that we are seconds away from freedom. But a loud crash above our heads forces my eyes up. I see the ceiling collapse and fall down all around us.

Covering Oscar as best I can, the debris hits my back. It's another miracle that we aren't crushed by it. But even though we survive, one thing is clear.

Our escape route is blocked. Between us and the door is a new wall of fire.

'No,' I mutter, wondering what I ever did to deserve all this bad luck.

Looking around, it seems as if the fire is blocking every possible avenue out of here. Now, despite all the other bleak moments, it feels like this might actually be the end.

'Karen!'

The loud call from somewhere inside this house has me looking around desperately, but I can't see anyone. It's just fire and smoke and crumbling brickwork.

And then I see him.

My husband, bursting through the flames with his arm outstretched, urging me to grab his hand.

I take it, and the strength of his grip reassures me amidst this chaos. He tries to pull me back the way he just came. But I'm reluctant to go that way, mainly because he's dragging me towards the fire, and there has to be a better way out than that, doesn't there?

Peter registers my hesitation and turns back to us, and when he does, he gathers me and Oscar in closely to him so he can be heard over the sound of the roaring flames.

'We have to go this way. If we're quick, then we'll be through the fire in a split second.'

'We can't. What about Oscar?' I look down at my frightened boy gripping my hand.

'Trust me. This is the only way out of here. We can do it.'

'We can't!'

'I'm not leaving you behind!'

I can see that Peter is serious. Not only did he run back into this burning building to find us, but he is refusing to go unless we do what he says.

'We can do it. I promise,' he tells me, and despite all the chaos around us, the look in his eyes somehow makes me feel as if everything is going to be alright.

'Okay,' I say, nodding, and he nods too before picking up Oscar.

'Close your eyes and keep your head down,' he tells our son before giving him a kiss and pulling him into his chest. Then he takes my hand and tells me that he loves me.

'I love you too,' I say in response.

Then he pulls me towards the fire.

It seems like we're facing a certain death, but I know Peter wouldn't take us this way unless he thinks we can make it.

The heat from the flames is overwhelming, and for a second the only thing I see is a blinding white light, but then the temperature drops suddenly, and I see something other than a fiery hell. I see green fields and white sheep and a brilliant, blue sky that is the most beautiful thing I think I've ever seen in my life.

We made it.

We're out of the house.

We survived.

I make sure to check on Oscar first, ensuring he is breathing properly and that his leg is okay. He says it hurts, but I reckon he got away without breaking it, although we'll need to go to hospital to get that confirmed. Then I look around for Noah, and while there is a brief moment of panic for me when I can't see him, I eventually spot him several feet away with a firefighter. Then I see several more firefighters rushing past us. One stops to ask us if there are any more people in the house.

I shake my head and hope that these brave souls will not risk their lives to check. It seems to be the case because they all stay put, aiming their hoses at the flames and dousing as much of the property in water as they can.

I hear a loud groan beside me. I turn to see Peter drop to the ground, clearly out of breath and exhausted from his exploits.

'Are you okay?' I ask him, kneeling beside him and checking for any injuries. But apart from being covered in soot and torn clothing, he seems to have escaped unscathed too.

'Yeah,' he mutters before spluttering for several seconds.

I look around for a paramedic who might be able to give my husband oxygen. But Peter gets his breathing back under control, and when he does, I wrap my arms around him and thank him for saving us.

Getting us all out of that basement was incredible, but running back into the house when he saw that Oscar and I were still inside was truly brave. There's no way we would have made it out without him. I kiss him and hug him and thank him again before I hear the sirens and see an ambulance arrive at the front of the house.

As I watch the paramedics climb out of their vehicle, I spot a man and a woman standing nearby whom I don't recognise. They seem distressed by what they are witnessing. But it's the person behind them who really gets my attention. She is being led towards the parked police car, struggling in handcuffs, trying to get away from the arresting officers.

It's a woman I recognise.

It's Eve, my friend, or at least a woman I thought was my friend until today.

Just before she is put into the car, she looks back and sees me watching her.

Does she smile? Frown? Shake her head?

No, she does none of those things. What she does is much worse. She just stares at me blankly, as if there is nothing between us. No history, no bond, no feeling.

It's as if I am dead to her.

But I'm not dead, and neither is my family. We made it out of this fire that was designed to take our lives, and now that we have, there is only one thing to do.

I need to speak to Eve. I need to get some answers.

41

EVE

I could get used to the routine of prison life. The wake-up calls, the meals and the lights out at the same time every day; seeing the same wardens presiding over the same prisoners; facing the same four walls day in and day out. I look around my cell and think about how this is the only life I will know for the next several years.

There is comfort to be found in routine, even if the routine isn't one you would pick for yourself. I guess this is why I feel like I will get used to prison life, which will make my sentence more bearable. It's a dreary world inside these walls, but it's not as if I've got anything or anyone waiting for me on the outside.

No family. No friends. *No place to live after I burnt it to the ground.*

I know I'm in this grim environment because I tried to kill an entire family. I accept that and own it, even if I did initially try to run away after Colin told the arriving police officers I was to blame for the blaze. But since being taken into custody I have calmed down, and I realise now that it is better if I don't try to pretend like I'm innocent. I knew exactly what I was doing and what the repercussions could be. That was why I pleaded guilty in court and started my sentence a lot quicker than if I fought it. I have nothing to hide anymore, and the truth can set me free, not literally of course, but internally at least.

I tried to kill Karen, Peter and those children, and for that I must pay.

But am I remorseful? No, because no matter what I did and whom I hurt, I still see Leanne's face when I close my eyes. And it's because of her that all this happened. Her suicide started this, and it will never end for me because she will never come back.

But today, there is a brief change to my routine.

That's because I have a visitor. Somebody has come to this prison to see me.

I hadn't expected her to actually turn up, but she did. When I walk into the visitors' room with the prison warden by my side, I see her sitting in the chair at the table.

'Hi, Karen,' I say calmly as I take a seat opposite the woman I tried to kill. She looks well considering only twelve weeks have passed since she was forced to fight for her life. If anything, I feel like I look worse for my time in here. That's because I'm wearing no makeup, eating terrible food and have no chance of getting a proper night's sleep, while she's been living her life – or as normal a life as it can be after I burnt her house to the ground.

Karen doesn't say anything to me at first, and I wonder if this might end up being a quick visit. But then she finally speaks, and when she does, she says something surprising.

'I think I'll be able to forgive you one day.'

'What?'

'For what you did. I think there will come a time when I can forgive you and move on. I'm a long way from it, but I know it will happen. For my sake, I hope it does.'

'I tried to kill you.'

'I know that.'

'And your family.'

'Yes, you did.'

'And you want to forgive me?'

'It's either that or hate you and be consumed by anger forever. But I don't want that. I don't want to be like you.'

That's when I realise what Karen is getting at. She is trying to show that she can be the bigger person here and not succumb to an overwhelming desire for revenge. She wants me to see that she is something I will never be.

Happy.

I guess that's her way of trying to prove that she won and I lost.

But there are no winners here, at least as far as I can tell.

'Why didn't you leave him?' I ask Karen, glancing at the silver ring on her left hand. 'He had an affair. How could you stay with him after that?'

Noticing I'm looking at her ring, Karen puts her hands on her lap, underneath the table and out of sight.

She says, 'I made the decision after considering what was best for me and my family.'

'Really? It just seemed like it was best for Peter. He avoided an expensive divorce, and he also had all that fun on the side while you were at home, looking after the kids.'

'What happened in our marriage was our business, not yours.'

'That's where you're wrong. It became my business when my best friend killed herself because of the coward you call a husband.'

I'm trying to rile Karen up and provoke a strong reaction in her, even if it's only because it would be nice to see her struggle just as much as I am. But I don't get the response I am looking for. Instead, she remains calm.

'I know what happened, and I know why you did all of this,' Karen says. 'And you were very clever with it all too. You tricked me, you tricked Peter, and you almost got what you wanted. But now it's over, and all you have done is spoil the memory of your best friend, who would never have wanted you to do all of this in her name.'

It's me who loses my composure, but I don't care. 'How would you know that? You never even met her! She would still be here if your husband hadn't broken her heart.'

'He broke *my* heart, and I'm still here.'

Karen stares at me, and while I would love nothing more than to reach across this table and grab her by the hair, I don't. Because now she has put it like that, I see that she and Leanne are not all that different. They both got messed around by Peter. It's just that Leanne was weak and did something that couldn't be repaired.

'So that's it, then, is it? You continue to play happy families and never think about the lives that were ruined?'

'There's no such thing as happy families,' Karen tells me sternly. 'There's just families, and they all have their problems. The important thing is that they stick together; my family does that. Maybe if you spent less time coming after us and more time starting a family of your own, you might have seen that there is still plenty of good in this world.'

Karen looks towards the prison warden and nods. She is ready for this visit to end. But I'm not quite ready for it to be over.

I lean across the table and whisper into her ear before the warden reaches us.

'You might one day be able to forget about me and what I did, but you'll never be able to forget what Peter did. That feeling of a broken heart never leaves a person. Trust me. I know as well as you do what it's like when the person you love is gone forever. I lost Leanne, and while Peter isn't dead, you know he's not the same man you married. Not after what he did. Good luck with that.'

I pull back and see a flicker of emotion on Karen's face. The warden orders me to stand up, and we make our way over to the door and the corridor that will take me back to my cell. When I turn back to look at Karen, she is still sitting in her chair and watching me leave.

In that moment I know she won't be back here again.

This will be the one and only visit we have, and because of that, I guess I'll miss her.

I'll miss her because she knows what I do.

She knows that there are some things that can't be forgiven.

And because of that, revenge will always be on her mind, no matter how often she tells herself to move on.

EPILOGUE
KAREN

My family and I could be forgiven for not wanting to set foot in any new houses for a while. But we have no choice if we want to find a new place to live. Now that the insurance has paid out on our house fire, the search for our next home has begun in earnest.

Rather than try to rebuild what we lost in the fire, we came to the collective decision that it would be best to start afresh in a new part of town, where we can make new memories that won't be clouded by what happened in the past. Not only was our last house the one that a deranged arsonist burnt to the ground, but it was also the place where I found out about Peter's affair. I'd be lying if I said I wasn't looking forward to leaving any reminders of that particular time in my life behind.

'Mum, these bedrooms are huge!' Noah cries, and his statement gives me mixed emotions. I'm happy that he likes this place, because his father and I like it too, and we are considering putting in an offer if it gets the kids' seal of approval. But I also feel a slight tug in my heart. Recently, my eldest stopped calling me 'Mummy' and shortened it to the much more adult 'Mum'.

It's yet another reminder that my children are growing up fast – not that I needed another one. Both Noah and Oscar did a lot of maturing over these last several months. I was afraid that they might both need counselling after what they went through after we escaped from that burning house. But while they displayed incredible resilience in getting back to normality, there were a few noticeable changes in their personalities. The biggest one was that they don't misbehave and cause problems for me and Peter half as often as they did before the ordeal.

I guess I can't really complain if the worst thing to come out of all this is better behaved kids. One thing is for sure; neither Noah nor Oscar deliberately lock themselves in bathrooms anymore.

'I think they like it,' Peter says to me. He puts his arm around my shoulder and gives me a smile while we make our way through our potential next home.

'I think so too,' I reply when I see Noah and Oscar run out of one room before darting into another. The pair are exploring this house as quickly as they can. No doubt they are picking out the best bedrooms for themselves, because if we do buy it, then they will want to stake their claim now.

We pause by the upstairs landing window that looks over the town we call home.

'So what do you say? Shall we put an offer in?' Peter asks me.

There are no views of rolling green hills here, nor are there sheep grazing in the fields, but that's just fine by us. A view of the countryside would only remind us of that cursed place. I'll happily take this panoramic view of buildings and busy roads over that any day. I'll also happily take the better place in our relationship Peter and I are in because, despite all we have been through, I feel like things have never been better.

Eve was right in what she said when I visited her in prison. Peter is not the same man I married. I know more about his weaknesses and capacity to cause pain to a loved one, and that will never leave me. But I also know how strong and brave he is; I witnessed it when he ran through the inferno to drag me and Oscar out of that house.

I saw how willing he was to do anything to protect us. I know he would lay down his own life for his wife and kids. That something will also never leave me, and when all those things are put together, I know what kind of man I married.

He is a man who is far from perfect, but he is also, at his core, a good person who would do anything for his family. That to me is the thing that matters the most.

'I think we should go for it,' I tell Peter. The kids run down the stairs and past the estate agent, who has been giving us a little privacy. 'Let's do it.'

Peter smiles at me before we go downstairs and let the estate agent know that we are interested, and that she and her client will be hearing from us very soon. Then the four of us leave, climbing back into our car before Peter drives us away, back through town, back to my mum and dad's house, where we are still living, but hopefully not for much longer.

It feels like we are finally closing one very long and very dark chapter in our lives, and soon we will be starting a new one, one that will be better than anything that came before it. But as I follow my family up the driveway back to my parents' house, I find myself glancing down the street.

Is there someone there with a camera? Are they taking photos of me and my loved ones right now? Are they conspiring against us, plotting revenge for things that happened in the past?

No, of course not. There is nobody there.

What happened with Eve was a one-off, and as long as she is in prison, we will be okay. There is no one else out to get us. No one else to tell us lies and lure us to dangerous places and trap us in rooms before starting a fire and standing back to watch.

It's all over now, and as I look at the empty street around me, I feel relieved that that is the case. Then I go inside the house. My children rush to tell their grandparents about the house they just saw, and Peter goes to the fridge to get a beer.

I close the front door behind me, but I don't lock it.

Even though it's getting dark and none of us will be going out again today, I leave it unlocked because, just like my kids, I haven't forgotten the feeling of helplessness of being trapped in that basement. Maybe that will change over time. I hope so. But for now I am leaving doors unlocked, in case I ever need to get away from something quickly.

That's ironic, I know. I'm aware this whole mess started because I felt like I had to get away from something. I needed a break from my family, and because of that I gave Eve the opportunity to lure us into her trap.

But I'm not going anywhere without my family again, and they aren't going anywhere without me.

There will be no more breaks.

ABOUT THE AUTHOR

Did you enjoy *The Break?* Please consider leaving a review on Amazon to help other readers discover the book.

Daniel Hurst writes psychological thrillers and loves to tell tales about unusual things happening to normal people. He has written all his life, making the progression from handing scribbled stories to his parents as a boy to writing full length novels in his thirties. He lives in the North West of England and when he isn't writing, he is usually watching a game of football in a pub where his wife can't find him.

Want to connect with Daniel? Visit him at his website or on any of these social media channels.

www.danielhurstbooks.com

ALSO BY DANIEL HURST

INKUBATOR TITLES

THE BOYFRIEND

(A Psychological Thriller)

THE PASSENGER

(A Psychological Thriller)

THE PROMOTION

(A Psychological Thriller)

THE NEW FRIENDS

(A Psychological Thriller)

THE BREAK

(A Psychological Thriller)

Printed in Poland
by Amazon Fulfillment
Poland Sp. z o.o., Wrocław
04 May 2022

41f74410-cc47-4620-982f-daae65afe05eR01